The

Dress-Up Mirror

The

Dress-Up Mirror

by

Raymond Bial

CRISPIN BOOKS

Crispin Books is an independent press based in Milwaukee, Wisconsin.
With its sibling imprint, Crickhollow Books, Crispin publishes quality fiction
and nonfiction for discerning readers.

For a complete list of books in print, visit:

www.CrispinBooks.com

or

www.CrickhollowBooks.com

Original Trade Softcover • ISBN: 978-1-883953-79-9

Summary: In this humorous story with supernatural elements, four young girls –
13-year-old Amanda, her younger sister Sally, and two friends visiting for a sleepover,
Josie and Roxanne – are transported through a magical portal into the past of their
small Midwestern town of Maysville, where they have to decide whether they should
get involved in a story of familial strife and ethnic prejudice.

The Dress-Up Mirror continues the amazing adventures of the Tucker sisters
and friends, begun in an earlier novel, a ghost story titled *Shadow Island:
A Spooky Tale of Lake Superior.*

This book is lovingly dedicated
to my four grandparents,
all of whom immigrated to this country
in the early twentieth century.
With dignity and honor they overcame
prejudice and discrimination
to make a new home for their families.

One of the proudest and
happiest days of their lives
was when they earned the
right to become American citizens.

I.

Amanda would be the first to admit that the trouble all began with the dress-up mirror. Of course, the anguished noises that penetrated their new home every night—desperate whispers that only she could hear—should also have been a warning that she and her family were in danger.

When her parents had bought the grand Victorian house early that summer, Amanda had been thrilled. Fringed with gingerbread trim, the stately two-story home had a wraparound porch, steep gables, cupolas, and a tower all covered by a gray slate roof. It had been built around the turn of the 19th century, from a design featured in a stylish magazine of the day.

Born and raised in Maysville, Amanda had always loved the old neighborhoods of her hometown. The blue-eyed girl with long honey-blond hair walked to school and the local library along tree-lined streets. She played in the city park and rode her bike downtown to go to the movies and stop for ice cream at the soda fountain on Main Street.

Her father, Steven Tucker, had never especially liked his job as an administrator at Thornton College, a small private school on the west side. But he had moved often as a child, and he wanted their children to grow up in "their own hometown." Amanda's father and her mother, Liddy Tucker, had both agreed long ago that Maysville would be a good place to raise a family.

Although Amanda's nine-year-old sister Sally and four-year-old brother Jacob could be pests, she had agreed with her parents. Maysville was pleasant—and safe—and she loved the comfortable home with all its spacious rooms, its many nooks and crannies, closets, and cubbyholes. She especially loved to read and hunker for hours over her art table that her parents had set up for her. And she often had parties and sleepovers with friends.

Through the warm summers, her family enjoyed cookouts and played badminton and croquet in the backyard. Amanda looked after her rabbits in their hutches, and with her father, she blasted contraband fireworks on the Fourth of July.

But lately Amanda had become restless. That May she had turned thirteen, and she realized, suddenly, that she lived in a mid-sized town in the Midwest where nothing ever happened. Just one word came to mind: *boring.*

Maysville might be a fun place for kids, but she was growing up. She had begun to imagine herself as a fashion designer living somewhere else, far away, in a ritzy apartment in a big city—maybe New York. Or even Paris.

But then her parents had bought the old Victorian. Having met and married while graduate students, Steven and Liddy Tucker had moved to Maysville and bought a bungalow when Amanda was still a baby. However, over the years, the little one-story had become cramped as the other Tucker children had come along. So, when the "For Sale" sign had gone up in front of the Victorian house, Amanda's parents had snatched it up.

The elegant house was just a few shady blocks from their bungalow on Lincoln Avenue, so Amanda enjoyed the thrill of moving to another place, without leaving her friends behind. And it was ideally located on a quiet brick street lined with towering trees and homes dating from the turn of the last century—right across the street from Ellsworth Park!

Her father explained to her how, in recent years, people had come to appreciate the historic character of the old neighborhoods of Maysville. They were fixing up the old houses. Over the years, the clapboards of the Victorians had been painted white or gray, but now folks were restoring the "painted ladies," as the houses were known, to their former glory with a combination of bright colors.

When their family friend and local architect Bill Reilly inspected the house, Amanda tagged along with her father. They strolled through the house as Mr. Reilly explained, "For Victorian homes, the colors ranged from deep, rich earth tones to bright jewel-like colors."

He went on to explain how the intricate scheme, often with two or more colors on the trim and clapboards, helped to highlight the ornamental design and interesting patterns of what he called "the gingerbread."

Mr. Reilly told her how people, like detectives, inspected paint chips and restored their homes to their original colors—inside and out. Most of the houses in their neighborhood now ranged from violet and purple hues to brick-red tones, along with pale greens, blues, and grays.

Their new house was just white, though, and kind of boring—like Amanda's parents. But with its clapboards and gingerbread trim, it was a pretty home, sunk in the shade of two towering oak trees in the front yard.

Bordered by white picket fences and laced with brick walks, the front and backyards had been laid out as English gardens. Just a scrap of green lawn remained in the backyard, along with a goldfish pond, and an old carriage house that had been converted into a garage years ago.

Mr. Reilly also admired the curved staircase that ascended from the living room to the second floor. "All hand-crafted," he said. "And these front rooms are impressive. Just look at the high ceilings, the flowery wallpaper, the oak woodwork." He really was excited by the home, and so were Amanda and her father.

The room to the left of the staircase was a study that opened to the screened-in porch that wrapped around the west side of the house. The living room, Amanda learned, was once called the parlor. It had a stone fireplace with a beautiful oak mantlepiece, trimmed with carved leaves and vines.

And Amanda was especially delighted with the crystal chandelier in the dining room. It made her feel elegant just to walk into the room.

They strolled into the old-fashioned kitchen, where Mr. Reilly pointed out, "It still has an iron sink and vintage faucets. There's also a walk-in pantry. And a back staircase to the second floor. And a separate hallway that loops back to the front rooms."

They continued along that hall to a couple of rooms on their right, probably a sewing room and servant's quarters, and then back to the study and parlor. Mr. Reilly pointed out how well the house had been maintained. "It's like stepping back in time—to more than a century ago. All the cabinets and counters, the oak trim around the window and doors, and the hardwood floors are original. There's been no damage anywhere other than that curious patch in the plaster wall near the front door."

"We wondered about that," Amanda's father admitted.

"It's hard to match the texture of the original plaster, but it was carefully repaired," Mr. Reilly explained as he ran his hand over the spot. "It would hardly be noticeable, if the rest of the house weren't so pristine."

"Any idea how it might have happened?" Amanda's father asked.

"Not a clue," Mr. Reilly chuckled. "That plaster sets as hard as rock, so someone must have taken a sledgehammer to it. Or blasted it with a cannon."

Mr. Tucker smiled. "That's what I like about these old houses. Each one has its own mystery. I always like to wonder who lived in these homes and what went on within their walls over the generations."

"You've certainly got a lot of history here," Mr. Reilly went on.

"But it's strange," Mr. Tucker confided. "The house has been kept like a museum, as if no one has actually lived here in decades. Someone must have lived here—there's at least a modern stove and refrigerator. But I couldn't even find out who owned the house. Seems it's been held in a private trust for ages—until those funds were exhausted, and the house had to be sold for back taxes."

"Probably a proud family of old money," Mr. Reilly speculated, "trying to hold on to the place as their wealth dwindled."

"According to the old city directories, the original owners were named Blackburn, but I haven't found out much about them yet," Mr. Tucker explained.

"Well, you got a beauty of a home," Mr. Reilly said as they

continued upstairs. "And I know you'll take good care of her."

The wide curved staircase wound up to a spacious hallway that led to four large bedrooms with walk-in closets, which amazed Mr. Reilly. "Closets were rare in those days. People usually kept their clothes in tall cabinets called wardrobes," he explained. "Closets were a sign of great wealth. And the ones in this home are so large." The closet in her parents' room was even lined with red cedar, which gave off a pleasant fragrance.

The bathroom had a claw-footed tub and a marble-topped vanity. Everything was made of the highest quality materials. There were other charming touches as well, such as the ornate wainscoting, leaded glass windows, stained glass fanlight over the front door, and the porcelain doorknobs.

"Whoever built this house must have had deep pockets," Amanda's father remarked.

"There were a lot of wealthy people in this town around the turn of the century," Mr. Reilly noted. "And whoever lived in this house must have been *very* rich."

Steven Tucker nodded. "With the zinc foundry, coal mines, brickyard, and railroads, Maysville was an affluent town back then, but the number of fine old homes here is still amazing."

"And all of them are finely crafted, like this old Victorian," Mr. Reilly pointed out. "I would have bought the house myself, if you hadn't beaten me to it."

The house stood on Elm Street, on the north edge of Ellsworth Park, in an old neighborhood of brick streets lined with round streetlamps that glowed softly in the evenings. The old-fashioned streetlamps also wound through the park, with its tall trees, wide lawns, and flowerbeds. It was Amanda's favorite park in Maysville. President Teddy Roosevelt had once addressed a crowd from the bandstand there, as a candidate of the Bull Moose Party.

Although the bandstand was long gone, the sprawling old park still had an elegant limestone pavilion, and had once had a goldfish pond with a fountain. But this graceful pool and fountain had since been converted to flowerbeds.

Amanda was overjoyed with the prospect of moving into her "new" home on Elm Street. With all its nooks, and crannies, it gave her plenty of "secret places" to get away from her annoying little sister and brother. Like her parents, she loved old houses. Something about them made her wonder just who had lived there before them.

But the very first night they moved there in midsummer, the house had been *spooky*. In the depths of the night, the old Victorian creaked and moaned, as if in agony. Shadows from tree branches, or something else, maybe human figures, swept across the windows and walls. Amanda felt very alone and far away in her large room on the second floor.

The next morning she stumbled downstairs and eased into the dining room where her family had gathered for breakfast.

Amanda rubbed her eyes and yawned. "Did you sleep all right?"

"Like a log," her father piped.

Her mother sighed. "As always, he was snoring away."

In the light of day, she asked her parents, "Uh, didn't you hear any strange noises last night?"

Her father chuckled, "Old house are always settling, honey. You'll get used to the night sounds."

"It's new place for you," her mother said. "And don't frighten your sister and brother."

With spoons poised over their cereal bowls, Sally and Jacob were already gazing back at her, wide-eyed and open-mouthed. Both had vivid imaginations, especially her kid sister, so Amanda simply agreed, "Sure, I guess it's just an old house doing what old houses do at night."

"And so charming," her mother gushed. " I can't believe we're actually living here!"

But that night Amanda again heard those creepy noises. She thought she heard restless footsteps—and voices too, as if people were quarreling in low tones. She was amazed that she finally drifted off to sleep, and was so relieved when she awoke to the morning light streaming into her room.

She hustled out of bed and sought out her father to speak with him alone. She found him in the study, hunkered over some financial report. He looked bored and was eager to take a break to talk with his older daughter.

"Noises again?" he asked, as if reading her mind.

Amanda nodded.

"It just takes time, honey," he assured her. And he told her once again, for the thousandth time, how his family had moved so often as he had been growing up. He had enjoyed the thrill of going to a new place, but had always missed his friends in the old home. "All things considered, your mother and I think it's better if you kids grow up here, among your friends and family, safe and sound in your own hometown."

But nothing about this creepy old house now felt *safe* or *sound.*

Oddly, no one else heard strange noises, so Amanda figured

she must be imagining the eerie sounds and shadows, like her scaredy-cat of a sister usually did. Unless, of course, she, Amanda Tucker, had been singled out.

Nothing bad happened, though, and, as she lay in bed, Amanda never saw...dare she even think it? She never saw a ghost. But the strange noises—shuffling, scraping, mumbling, and an occasional knock—became more frequent and intense.

This went on for a whole restless week. And then another.

Now *boring* had been replaced by *terrifying*.

Every night Amanda lay awake, anxious and afraid.

One morning she'd had enough. She spoke to her parents again.

"You're hearing the normal noises of an old house and letting your imagination get the best of you," her mother suggested.

"Our room is just down the hall," her father assured her. "Why don't you come get us, if any noises frighten you again."

"And we'll look in on you, honey," her mother added.

Amanda felt like a little kid again. She was too embarrassed to say that she had heard voices, too, or at least thought she had. And those shadows that slipped along the walls looked so ...human.

She reminded her parents that last summer while on vacation, her little sister Sally, her best friend Roxanne, and she had gotten trapped on an island out on Lake Superior. And ghosts had definitely haunted Shadow Island.

But her father assured her, "That was a remote place far away from here, Amanda." He chuckled. "Haven't you been complaining that nothing ever happens in Maysville?"

As she curled up in bed that night, Amanda told herself that she was too old to be frightened by noises. Wasn't she the big sister in this family? But she had this strange feeling that others, besides her own family, inhabited this old house. Could ghosts be haunting these rooms? If so, it seemed they didn't appreciate the Tuckers living here.

On Friday night there were more noises, loud and frantic, throughout the night. Amanda heard muffled shrieks of "Murder! Murder!" and some sort of quarreling about a mirror. She looked around the dark bedroom, petrified. Amanda wanted to flee to her parents' room, but how weird would that be? She was thirteen. She wasn't a kid anymore. And maybe she was just dreaming. It was silent now. Amanda waited, but there were no more sounds. Exhausted, she finally fell asleep.

In the morning, however, Amanda scrambled out of bed and hustled down the ornate staircase to the dining room.

It was another hazy day in early August, a quiet Saturday morning in Maysville, and Amanda was so relieved to find her parents at the breakfast table chatting in their light-hearted way—about an antique mirror.

"I know it's a lovely mirror, Liddy," her father chuckled. "But I can't believe you paid two hundred dollars for it!"

"It was for a good cause," her mother said. "The annual fundraiser at the county historical museum."

A full-length oval mirror with scalloped edges stood in the corner of the dining room. It was held upright on a mahogany stand by brass hinges so that it could tilted forward or backward.

"It's an antique," Liddy Tucker went on. "I thought it would make a lovely house-warming present for ourselves."

"We've already sunk a fortune into this house," Steven

moaned. "We have to be careful with our expenses."

A delicate woman with dark brown hair and eyes, Liddy touched her fingertips to her forehead. "I know, but I couldn't resist bidding on that mirror. You'll laugh, but I felt drawn to it."

Amanda had been desperate to tell her parents about the noises, but now she longed to put the night terrors out of her mind, at least for the moment. As she eased into the room, she put on a pleasant face and exclaimed, "What a beautiful mirror! Where did you find it, Mom?"

"I was out for my morning walk," Liddy Tucker explained. "It's strange, because I don't usually walk that way, but I passed by the historical museum, and they were having an open house and auction for all kinds of antiques. I stepped inside and saw lots of lovely items. But like your father says, money is tight for us now. So I just poked around a little, and I was about to leave when I noticed this mirror. For some reason, I just had to have it, and I could have gotten it for a song, except this old man kept bidding against me. I do believe he would have paid any price for the mirror, even a thousand dollars, but he hadn't brought enough cash and the auctioneer wouldn't extend credit. Luckily I had my checkbook with me. I have to say it was odd how mad that old man became when I got the mirror."

"Mad?" Amanda asked.

Liddy nodded. "Furious. He offered to buy the mirror from me—said he'd give me double the price I'd paid. But he was so nasty and annoying that I didn't want to have anything to do with him. He made quite a scene. He got so angry his face turned purple, and he ranted that the mirror was cursed and I'd be sorry. He raised his cane, and I thought he was going to hit me. But instead he lunged at the mirror and yelled, 'I have to shatter it once and for all!'"

Amanda and her father were speechless.

Liddy continued, "Fortunately, some men rushed forward and restrained him. They called the police, but I didn't want to press charges—he's just a poor, senile old man. The police escorted him from the museum. Everyone apologized, saying the man's family had lived in Maysville for generations, although curiously no one knew him well—he apparently keeps to himself. They assured me that he'd always been mild and painfully shy. He certainly had never acted that way before."

"That mirror is probably jinxed," Steven joked. "If I look into it, maybe I'll go cross-eyed. Or my hair will fall out."

Amanda couldn't pass up the chance to kid her father. "Don't you mean the *rest* of your hair, Dad?"

"It's so strange that the old man claimed the mirror is cursed," Liddy chuckled. "Can you believe such a silly thing? In this day and age?"

Amanda asked, "Where did the mirror come from originally?"

"That *is* a mystery," her mother said, shaking her head. "Nobody at the historical museum could tell me. Apparently, one morning someone left it by the front door with a note, saying that it was a donation to be auctioned off."

"An anonymous donor," Amanda wondered. "Who it could be?"

"Many generous people don't like to draw attention to themselves," Mrs. Tucker explained. "Like the person who always slips a gold coin in the Salvation Army bucket just before Christmas."

"It *is* a fine mirror," Steven acknowledged. "And it goes perfectly with the house, as if it belongs here. It appears to be from the same time period—turn of the century. But may I ask one question?"

"What?" Liddy asked cautiously.

"Uh, where do you intend to put this mirror?"

Although the Tuckers had just moved into the house, it already seemed quite full with books, toys, photographs, and keepsakes, besides all their furniture—not to mention the computers and large-screen television that were the special love of techno-whiz Sally, who at the moment was shoveling down another bowl of cereal in the living-room. Amanda was sure Sally had her eyes glued to an episode of Saturday morning cartoons, in between emailing or texting friends on her laptop and cell phone.

Gazing at the antique mirror, Amanda had an idea. "How about the attic?" she suggested.

"The attic?" her parents asked simultaneously.

"It would be perfect for dress-up," Amanda explained. "I've already got all my old clothes and a lot of other stuff up there."

"Just how did you get dibs on the attic?" her dad asked. "I had my eye on that space for a writing room."

"Besides, the mirror will be perfect for my sleepover tonight."

"Sleepover?" Steven asked.

"Tonight?" Liddy inquired. "I don't recall your asking to have a sleepover."

"That's because I just came up with the idea. So we haven't talked about it—yet," Amanda said. "How about it, Mom? Dad? It will only be Josie and Roxanne."

Her mother reflected for a moment. "You haven't been sleeping well. Maybe a sleepover isn't a good idea. You need to get some rest."

"Trust me, Mom," Amanda said. "A sleepover is just what I need."

Her father shrugged. "Might be a good idea, Liddy. It might help Amanda get accustomed to this creaky old house."

"That's right!" Amanda said.

Not only would she *not* have to sleep in her spooky room, she would not be alone tonight. And maybe she could forget this strange mystery, at least for one night.

"What about your little sister?" Amanda's father asked. "You're going to let Sally join you, aren't you?"

"Aw, Dad!"

Of course, her mother chimed in. "You know, how Sally adores you and doesn't like to be left out."

"But she's *my sister,*" Amanda said, as if that explained it all.

"You know how much she likes your friends, and they are so fond of her."

"Ha!" Amanda snorted. "Sally is *always* bugging them—and me. Besides, she's just a little kid. And my friends don't have to live with her. They don't know her like I do."

"She's nine years old," Steven reminded her. "It's not like when she was young and always getting into your stuff."

"She still gets into my stuff. And under my skin," Amanda grumbled.

At that moment, Sally Tucker, tomboy and troublemaker, at least in Amanda's eyes, ambled toward the kitchen for another bowl of cereal—probably her third or maybe her fourth. There must be a commercial on TV, Amanda thought, because otherwise Sally wouldn't so much as glance away from the screen.

For a moment, the sisters eyed each other. They had gotten along better over the past year, since that strange and frightening night on Shadow Island. But Amanda still thought that they were opposites. She and her brown-eyed sister might both have the same honey-blond hair, but the similarity ended there. Sally loved sports and technology, while Amanda had always shied away from competition and computers, preferring books and traditional arts, like painting and drawing. Amanda was growing into a slender, elegant young lady, while Sally delighted in thumping all comers, including boys—*especially* boys—in soccer, baseball, and basketball.

"Come on, Amanda," Sally beseeched her sister. "Can I?"

"Can you what?" Amanda snorted. "You don't even know what we're talking about."

"Do too!"

"What is it then?"

"Uh, you're going to ride your bikes to the swimming pool?"

"Nope."

"You're going to the Custard Corner for ice cream cones?"

"Nope."

"The library?"

"Nope."

Sally cocked a doubtful eye at her, since everyone knew that Amanda always had her nose stuck in a mystery novel or history book and had once again won the summer reading contest at the Maysville Carnegie Library.

A knowing gleam sparkled in her brown eyes. "A sleepover! We're having a sleepover!"

"Correction. *I* am having a sleepover," Amanda said. "And you're not invited."

"I live here, too," Sally pointed out. "I can sleepover at my own house whenever I want to."

"You can sleepover in your own room, or in the bathtub or under the kitchen table!" Amanda said. "*Not* up in the attic with us. We're going to do dress-up. You're too young. You'd just get in the way. And you're too…hyper. You'd just make a mess of all the clothes."

"Amanda," Mrs. Tucker said firmly. "You may have a sleepover, as long as you include your little sister."

"Aw, Mom!"

"And you must be kind to her," Mr. Tucker added.

"Aw, Dad!"

"And Sally will agree to behave herself," Mrs. Tucker said.

"That's impossible," Amanda grumbled. "It's against her nature."

"It is not!" Sally spat out.

"Is too!"

"Girls!" Mrs. Tucker pleaded.

"Enough," Steven Tucker said. "Amanda…Sally…You heard your mother."

Rising from the table, he sighed. "I'll carry the mirror upstairs."

II.

Although she had lived in the Victorian home for only a short while, Amanda had already claimed several spaces for herself—her second-floor bedroom, of course, but also an art table down in the finished basement, which the Tuckers had made into a family room. Longing to become a fashion designer, she was methodically working her way through the girls' names from A to Z in a "what to name the baby" book. For hours, Amanda drew pictures of models with names from Abby to Zora, each in a stylish outfit, including accessories—hats, purses, shoes, and jewelry.

She also liked to read mystery novels while curled up in a cushioned seat built into a second-floor alcove in the turret as the sun streamed through the tall windows.

Of all the cozy places in the old house, however, Amanda most loved the attic, which she had claimed as her fashion studio with an easel, drawing pads, and racks of old clothes that she and her mother had picked up at vintage clothing shops.

Amanda thought that she and her friends could use the attic as a hangout—away from her pest of a kid sister. However, with its dark corners and the strange noises that percolated through the house, she avoided the attic at night. And she did *not* want to have a sleepover up there. But where else in the old house? Certainly not her own room, which was racked with those anguished groans.

At that point, Amanda wasn't sure if she should have a sleepover *anywhere* in the old house, especially now that Sally had invited herself. And she might have abandoned the idea, except that her friend Josie had bugged her so often—every day since the Tuckers had moved. Time and again, the tall, willowy girl had said, "Come on, Amanda, you've lived here like how long? Weeks now! We need to have a sleepover."

Amanda hoped that the house might not be so scary at night if she were with friends. But she felt guilty about inviting her two best friends over, especially Roxanne, and wondered if she should tell them about the voices that had become so frantic in the middle of the night. Roxanne especially was so timid; she'd be terrified, although she claimed not to believe in ghosts.

Josie on the other hand was fearless. Most likely she would want to flush out the ghosts and unravel this mystery.

I'll keep it my secret, Amanda concluded, and we'll just curl up in sleeping bags downstairs on the living-room floor and watch movies on TV.

Late that afternoon her friends appeared at the house, carrying their bags of clothes and all the other things needed for a sleepover. "It's about time!" outspoken Josie said as she walked in the door.

"I'm starved," Roxanne said.

Soon, the three girls were hunkering over the dining-room

table and feasting on delivered pizzas loaded with sausage, pepperoni, mushrooms, and double cheese.

"I see you girls got the works," Amanda's father chuckled as he glanced at the triangular slabs piled with toppings.

Josie, who had been unabashedly wolfing down one wedge after another, responded, "Hey, Mr. Tucker, I'm a growing girl."

And she *was* shooting up, and becoming more graceful than ever.

As always, Sally insisted on having her own pizza—pepperoni only—which she ate by herself on the sofa, in front of the television, so she wasn't there to bug Amanda, Roxanne, and Josie, at least not yet.

Amanda wondered if she should confide in her friends about the frightening noises. However, dark-haired Roxanne was scared of her own shadow. While Amanda tended to be a little dreamy and even romantic, her friend was practical and analytical when it came to the supernatural. She didn't believe in ghosts, not for a moment. But she was still terrified of them.

Tall and lanky, Josie towered over Roxanne. As goalkeeper in soccer and center on the basketball team in middle school, she loved a good fight. Josie's green eyes and curly auburn hair seemed to belie her fiery and adventurous spirit.

"It's my Irish temper," Josie often joked.

She and Roxanne were polar opposites, and Amanda was often caught in the middle. Nonetheless, the three girls were best friends and an interesting mix, especially now that they had started to become interested in boys.

As always, Sally was the wild card in the mix.

After demolishing two extra-large pizzas, the three friends sagged in their chairs.

Roxanne declared, "I cannot believe you ate a whole pizza, Josie."

"Did I?"

"Yes!"

"But I thought I saved a slice for you."

"Nope," Amanda said. "Roxanne and I split the other pizza. I don't know where you put it all."

"That's funny," Josie said. "And I'm still a little hungry."

"My sister probably ate a whole pizza, too," Amanda chuckled.

Josie shrugged. "Guess Sally and I need our energy for soccer and softball."

"So where are we going to have our sleepover?" Roxanne asked.

Amanda suggested the living room, where they could watch movies and eat popcorn, to which Josie responded, "Boring! How about your attic?"

"Attic?" Amanda sighed.

"Yep," Josie said. "You told me how cool it is, remember, with all those old clothes. We can play dress-up."

"That would be fun," Roxanne agreed.

"But my sister might be joining us," Amanda countered. "And you know Sally. She'll just throw clothes around the attic and make a mess."

"I like your little sister," Josie said. "She's cool."

"Right," Amanda said, "except when her imagination goes wild and she gets scared of every little thing."

"Yeah, even better," Josie exclaimed. "Once it gets dark, it'll be so spooky up there! Perfect!"

"I don't know about that," Roxanne muttered.

"Don't be a baby," Josie said. "If it gets too scary for you, we'll just come back downstairs and watch a dumb movie."

Amanda had run out of excuses, unless she told them about the noises that had been keeping her awake late into the night, and that would just make it worse. So after they stacked their plates, utensils, and the greasy pizza boxes next to the sink, the three of them scrambled up the stairs to the third-floor attic.

It was late in the day. The attic felt suddenly creepy to Amanda, especially after climbing the flight of dark, narrow stairs that led up there. Each step had creaked underfoot.

As the girls began to play dress-up, it was comforting for Amanda to know that her parents were close by. Her father was surely looking over papers in his study, and her mother was probably outside, yanking weeds in the gardens of heirloom flowers in the backyard.

Best of all, there were no strange noises or voices in the attic—at least not yet—and she was having fun with her friends. Even her hellcat of a little sister had not pestered them. There must be some thrilling show on television: maybe another daredevil reality show or a preseason Chicago Bears football game.

Ever since she'd been a toddler and had begun motoring around the house, Sally had raised a constant ruckus, getting into Amanda's art stuff or tearing around the house, declaring, "I'm hyper! I'm hyper!" Sally was such a fearless spitfire in sports that she could have played fullback for the Chicago Bears. But curiously the high-voltage girl was petrified by the supernatural: ghosts, goblins, witches, vampires, and whatever else she imagined. You name it.

She wasn't too crazy about snakes and spiders either.

Amanda smiled to herself. Sally must be too scared to venture up into the attic, especially now that a veil of dusk was settling over them. Amanda glanced over at the big mirror, set off to the side. It looked quite charming up there, resting on its stand.

No sooner had that pleasant thought occurred to her than Amanda looked into the mirror and—speak of the daredevil— she saw her kid sister appear in the doorway behind her.

"Hi," Sally called out cheerfully.

"Hi," Josie and Roxanne echoed her.

Amanda scowled.

Anxious about saying or doing something wrong around Amanda and her friends, Sally eased into the room, while the other girls turned back to rummaging in a couple of big boxes of dress-up clothes and pulling old vintage dresses off a rack that was set up in a corner. With delight, they took turns trying on weird combinations of oversized dresses, clunky shoes, floppy hats, and other accessories.

Hoping to be included in the activities of the older girls, Sally was being especially polite, even timid. Keeping her distance, she quietly draped herself in an outrageous mix of a colorful old dress, a flowery hat, several scarves, and a pair of high-heels.

Amanda had to smile as she glanced at Sally. Her little sister favored blue jeans or bib overalls in cool weather, and cotton shorts and t-shirts through the other seasons. She couldn't recall the last time, if ever, that her sister had worn a dress or a skirt and blouse.

But now the tomboy terror was trying to doll up like a lady. Amanda imagined that her sister would next want to apply lipstick, rouge, and mascara generously onto her face.

There were vintage clothes hung on racks and piled in boxes around the attic, so the girls could choose from an array of garments. Most of the dresses, hats, and shoes had been accumulated over the years, because their mother never threw anything away. There were not only clothes from Liddy Tucker's childhood, but old dresses, skirts, blouses, shoes, hats, and jewelry from their grandmothers.

As a budding fashion designer, Amanda had lately been able to talk her mother into occasionally stopping by the vintage clothing stores in town: *Secondhand Rose, Daisy's Vintage Shop,* and *Rags and Riches.* Mrs. Tucker, Amanda, and even Sally also loved yard sales, and they had picked up many bargains on Saturday mornings, so Amanda had acquired her own wardrobe of old clothes from the 1930s to the 1970s.

The girls rummaged through the trunks and boxes, delighting in the variety of feathery hats and flowery dresses. As they gussied themselves up, hooting at each other's outrageous outfits, they gathered around the full-length oval mirror held upright on its mahogany stand.

As she slipped on an old straw hat with floppy brim and wild flowers stuck on the top, Amanda realized that she, too, was having fun, even as the night deepened around them.

No sooner had she enjoyed that thought than, in the next moment, she once again heard the faint creaking sounds, as if an invisible person—or perhaps several lost souls—were wandering restlessly through the house.

Oh no.

Amanda was seized with terror. Until now, she had only heard the creepy noises in her own room. Maybe they should go downstairs and watch a movie, she thought. But her friends and little sister were having so much fun chattering to each other as they trotted around in the fancy old dresses and oversized high heels that she didn't want to frighten them. Yet Amanda couldn't put the noises out of her mind—and they were all the more terrifying because no one else seemed to hear them!

The light of a full moon now angled through the small, diamond-shaped windows, and a gloom pervaded the attic room.

Maybe if I turn on a lamp, it will scare them away or at least quiet the noises, Amanda thought. She was reaching over to pull the string on a floor lamp with bronze pole and fringed shade when she noticed a smudge on the mirror, like a fingerprint. Now how did that get there? Sally must have mucked it up, she thought, while I had my back turned.

Snapping a Kleenex from the box on a wobbly table near an old leather-strapped trunk, she reached over to wipe the smudge away and to her amazement, her fingertips slipped into the mirror, disappearing, as if the glass were liquid, like water.

Amanda snatched her hand back, shocked.

That could not have happened, she told herself. It is simply not possible. She glanced at Josie and Roxanne, but they were so busy tugging some long, striped stockings on Sally that they hadn't noticed her.

Amanda tried to speak to them, but she couldn't make her mouth form any words. *No, no, no! They'll think I'm crazy. Josie will laugh at me and Roxanne will be scared to death,* she thought, as the noises swirled around her. Amanda hesitantly reached forward to touch the silver surface of the mirror. Her trembling fingers again slipped through the glass, as if it were nothing, until her whole hand vanished.

In terror, she yanked her hand back.

"Hey, Amanda!" Josie called over to her. "Once we get all dolled up, let's go down to the bathroom and put on make-up.

Your parents won't mind, will they?"

Sally giggled, "Not as long as they're asleep!"

"What's the matter?" Roxanne asked. "You look as white as a sheet, Amanda. Like you've seen a ghost."

"Ghost?" Sally gasped, her brown eyes widening as she glanced around the dark corners of the attic.

Amanda gulped, "Uh, guys, you…you…you will not believe this."

She pushed her hand through the mirror; then snatched it back.

Josie and Roxanne could not comprehend the strange phenomenon. They stared at each other.

"Hey, that is so cool!" Josie exclaimed. "Like magic."

"How'd you do that, Amanda?" Roxanne asked, herself looking more than a little frightened.

"I'm scared," Sally whispered.

"Do it again!" Josie urged. "What is it…some kind of optical illusion? What a great trick!"

Her throat dry, Amanda barely managed to speak. "It's not a trick. I don't know how or why…it just happened."

"Yeah, right," Josie snorted.

"Where's Mom?" Sally asked.

"Of course there's a logical explanation," Roxanne snapped. "So quit playing jokes on us, Amanda."

"Yeah, you're just trying to scare us!" Sally burst out. "You're *mean*, Amanda. I'm gonna tell Mom and Dad."

The little girl marched over to the mirror and shoved the palm of her hand against what she must have expected to be a hard surface. Her arm plunged through the glass all the way to her elbow. Sally studied the mirror and her submerged arm for a moment. Then, in shock and terror, she snatched her arm back.

"How'd you do that?" Josie asked.

Sally just stood there, her mouth hung open.

Josie slipped her hand into the mirror and quickly withdrew it, muttering, "This is so cool."

"It's impossible," Roxanne contended. "It must be a trick mirror from a magician's act."

"Come on," Josie urged. "You try it."

Roxanne gasped. "No...No way!"

"It doesn't hurt," Josie said.

Roxanne had a look of horror on her face, as did Sally. They were all middle-class girls living in a mid-sized town in the Midwest. Beyond the island of trees, which composed the landscape of Maysville, were rolling cornfields, pastures, and nothing more than other small towns, just like their own. Their town was supposed to be boring.

The girls went to movies and hung out downtown. They watched television, spent hours on the computer, and read books about exciting places, including stories about ghosts and other supernatural phenomenon. But nothing exciting or mysterious ever *really* happened in their hometown.

"Why is the mirror doing this?" Roxanne whispered.

"And why is it doing it *now?*" Amanda wondered out loud, recalling how her mother, earlier that day, had worked out in the garage to clean the mirror thoroughly before she'd let Steven carry it to the attic. As was Liddy's nature, she had "put some elbow grease into it," polishing the wood and rubbing the glass until it sparkled.

And nothing had happened then.

Even now, as the four perplexed girls stared at it, it appeared to be no more than an antique mirror with a normal silvery pane that reflected their faces and portions of the dusky light of the attic.

When they had moved into the Victorian house, the Tuckers had cleaned the house and aired out every room, including the attic. Had that action—kicking up the dust of the old house—released some magic that now had worked itself upon the mirror? Or had the simple act of placing the mirror *in* the house altered it? Or in the attic? Or maybe nightfall had prompted this strange phenomenon?

Was it the attic that was eerie? Or the mirror?

With an odd, tingly feeling, Amanda—and no doubt Sally, too—recalled their mother's story about the nasty man who had so desperately wanted the mirror, and how he had claimed that it was cursed and had tried to smash the antique.

Amanda related this story to Josie, who was bright-eyed with curiosity, and Roxanne, whose face was strained with a worried scowl.

"It *has* to be a gimmick," Roxanne suggested. "It must have been part of some magic act. Like those boxes where they cut women in half or make them disappear."

Quietly standing back, Sally did not seem convinced, while the other girls began to inspect the mirror more closely. Scarcely uttering a word, they ran their fingers along the edges of the scalloped frame. They next studied the back of the mirror, but nothing appeared unusual, just a lovely mahogany veneer that felt as solid as any wood when they tapped on it.

"It looks and feels just like any clunky old mirror," Josie concluded.

Swallowing hard and shivering a little, Roxanne suggested,

"We should tell your parents, Amanda."

However, Amanda and Josie had become so absorbed with the mirror that they couldn't take their eyes off it. Daringly, Josie eased her entire arm through the watery surface of the mirror, watching it vanish to the shoulder.

"I wonder what's in there," she reflected. "You know, on the other side."

"Could be anything," Amanda answered. "Or nothing."

Josie stuck her arm back in the mirror. "I can't feel anything."

Roxanne exclaimed, "For Pete's sake, get your arm out of there!"

Josie casually withdrew her arm. "It doesn't hurt or anything, Roxanne."

Amanda shoved both of her arms through the mirror. Then she stuck her right leg into the mirror, but she felt nothing other than a slightly cooler atmosphere on the other side.

"Come on, you guys," Roxanne begged, kneading her hands together. "Knock it off. This is too weird. Let's get out of here and tell your parents. Now!"

Ignoring her, Josie suggested to Amanda, "Why don't you look inside the mirror?"

"Me?" Amanda answered. "Why don't *you*?"

"Hey, this is your house," Josie countered, tossing her reddish-orange curls back over her shoulder. "And your mirror."

Roxanne stood silently, quivering, not saying a word.

Sally continued to hang back. She might have fled down the stair, except that, come nightfall, she never liked to be alone anywhere in the dark house, so she was sticking close to the older girls.

"What are you so worried about, Amanda?" Josie chided.

"Come on, just peek inside."

Amanda was curious, but mostly terrified. "What if my head gets stuck?"

For a moment, the girls stared at the mirror, then Sally stepped forward. Perhaps she hoped to relieve her fear by understanding this mystery or simply wanted to show up her sister. Before anyone could stop her, the little girl thrust her head through the liquid surface of the mirror.

"Sally!" Amanda cried, pulling her sister back so her head reappeared.

"What did you see?" Josie exclaimed.

"Nothing!" Sally muttered. "It's just gray—like a fog."

Annoyed at being outdone by her 'fraidy-cat of a kid sister and assured that it was possible to look inside and not get decapitated, Amanda leaned forward and peeked through the mirror.

She saw nothing beyond the mist that Sally had described. Amanda again felt that slightly cooler atmosphere, and she quickly backed out of the mirror.

"This is so strange," she whispered, short of breath.

"It's like some kind of movie," Roxanne observed. "This cannot *really* be happening—not to us, not in real life."

Feeling that she had to mention that harrowing night of ghostly encounters last summer on their vacation up north, Amanda said, "Remember what happened to us on Shadow Island. This could be another great adventure."

Roxanne turned white as a sheet, but Josie was thrilled. "This is the most amazing thing I've ever seen," she exclaimed, looking from one girl to the next. "I guess one of us will just have to climb all the way inside."

She paused. "Go ahead, Amanda."

"Me?" Amanda cried. "Why me? Don't tell me it's because it's my house."

Josie shrugged. "And your mirror."

Amanda mumbled, "Actually, it's my mom's mirror."

"But you're the one who discovered that it's magical," Josie pointed out.

Roxanne groaned. "This could be worse than Shadow Island, Amanda. We were lucky we got out of there alive."

"But we're safe at home now," Amanda said. "And like you said, there's got to be some logical explanation for this mirror."

"People have plenty of accidents at home," Roxanne pointed out. "More than anywhere else."

"Sally sure does," Amanda agreed.

This was true, mostly because her stunt sister was always racketing through the house at top-speed, often pretending to be a super heroine. For example, just a few years ago, their mother had once heard a loud clunk and rushed to the foot of the basement stairs. There lay Sally rubbing her knee.

"Are you okay?" Mrs. Tucker had asked.

"Yep."

"What happened?" their mother had asked.

"I jumped from the fifth step," Sally had explained.

"Why on earth would you do such a thing?"

"I was trying to fly like Superwoman," Sally had sighed. "But I couldn't."

But the nine-year-old daredevil also had a multitude of phobias—of the dark, spider and snakes, not to mention ghosts, ghouls, and especially zombies.

Although Sally looked fearful, she was overcome by curiosity too. It was such an oddity—it just had to be explored. In almost a whisper, she said, "I'll…I'll go in there."

"No you won't!" Amanda snapped, refusing to be outdone by her sister. Ever so carefully, she stepped in front of Sally and climbed inside the mirror, first her left leg and then her right. "Just hold onto me!" she told Josie, clasping her friend's hand. "No matter what, do not let go of me!"

Immediately, Amanda felt herself falling a couple of feet, until there was what appeared to be a solid floor beneath her feet. But it was so hazy on the other side of the mirror that she could see nothing.

Quickly, she climbed back through the mirror. "There's nothing in there," she reported.

"How can that be?" Josie asked. "There has to be something."

Roxanne said anxiously, "Come on, Amanda, we've got to tell your parents."

"You sound like a broken record," Josie grumbled. Turning to Amanda, she suggested, "Maybe you need to step inside *and* let go of me. You know, not hold onto anything."

"Not anything?" Amanda whispered, short of breath. "That's too scary."

"What's there to be afraid of?" Josie said. "Just go in, look around, and come right back out."

Not at all sure of herself, Amanda said, "What if I can't get back?"

Nobody had an answer for her.

Amanda might have stood there all night had not Sally drawn a long sigh and announced, "Then I'll do it, if you're such a scaredy cat."

"What's come over you?" Amanda exclaimed. "You're afraid of your own shadow!"

Sally shrugged. "Nothing bad has happened so far. I'll just—"

At that instant, there was a slow and ominous *click, click, click,* up the hardwood stairs that led to the attic…and toward the girls.

All four of them whirled around and stared in horror at the open doorway.

"What's that?" Sally gasped.

Roxanne cried, "It's coming after us!"

Amanda recalled the moans, creaks, and other strange sounds that seemingly arose from the very soul of this old house. Curiously, she realized that the noises had ceased at the very moment when she'd discovered the magic of the mirror…until now. Ghosts must inhabit this stately Victorian…and now they were converging on the four of them.

Instinctively, the girls all clung to each other.

"Some *thing* is coming up the stairs," Roxanne gasped. "And it's *not* your parents, Amanda."

Click, click, click.

"We've got to hide," Amanda exclaimed.

"Hide?" Josie snorted. She grabbed the floor lamp and raised it like a club. "I'll crack its skull."

A moment later, a long grizzled nose poked through the doorway, low to the ground, followed by the long body, swaying belly, and stubby legs of the Tuckers' old beagle. The dog was tri-colored—brown, black, and white—but now also gray, mostly around her face.

"Tulip!" Sally cried.

The girls sagged with relief.

Waddling over to the girls, the little dog stared at them with her sad, droopy eyes.

"What is she doing here?" Roxanne wondered.

Amanda didn't answer her.

Their old sausage of a dog rarely moved. The Regal Beagle was so lazy that she sometimes had to be carried outside to do her duty in the yard. Since moving into the new house, she had staked out two comfort zones—the kitchen and a cozy corner of the living room. Her life revolved around these two places: her food dish by the stove and a warm spot under the end table near the living-room fireplace. She never bothered to venture anywhere else in the house.

Tulip would never undertake the supreme effort of mounting a flight of stairs. However, she had now lumbered not only to the second floor, but all the way to the attic, like a mutt on a mission.

"Maybe she thinks we have some leftover pizza up here," Josie snorted.

Sally shook her head. "That's not like Tulip. She would just whimper until someone got up, delivered the pizza to her, and put it right in front of her nose. She acts like it's animal cruelty that she has to waddle all the way into the kitchen for her meals."

Her potbelly grazing the floorboards, Tulip toddled over to the mirror and sniffed the edges.

Then Her Highness the Hound *roofed*.

"Your dog is telling us something," Roxanne said. "And it's not 'Beware of the dog,' it's 'Beware of the mirror.'"

Although she knew that Roxanne was right, Amanda rolled her eyes. "My Mom put her on a diet—doctor's orders. Maybe she's so desperate for a handout that she climbed all the way up here."

"But she barked at the mirror!" Roxanne exclaimed.

Josie snorted. "More like wheezed."

With her brown, soulful eyes, the old dog gazed at the girls. She was a sweet and kindly mutt, although she never wagged her tail, which apparently took too much effort.

"Tulip is trying to warn us," Roxanne said.

"Then let's find out why!" Josie declared.

Roxanne was horrified. "Are you crazy?"

"It won't hurt to look around," Josie contended. "Amanda will just go through the mirror and poke around for a while. Then she can come back and tell us about it."

"Me again?"

"Sure!" Josie urged. "No big deal."

Amanda was scared. She felt an ominous presence—as if the spirits wandering the house had only gone mute to watch the girls. Were these ghosts dangerous to her family and to her friends? Amanda sensed that she had to solve this mystery or no one would ever be safe in this place.

Besides, there was no point in arguing with her stubborn friend. "I'll go," she sighed. "Just hold on to me until the last second. Okay, Josie?"

"Sure!"

Roxanne rubbed her hands together. "Come right back. Please!"

Amanda said nervously, "I'll just take a quick look and hustle out of there."

Once again, she stepped through the mirror, calling over her shoulder, "If I yell for help, come after me. Promise?"

The other girls glanced at each other.

"Uh, yeah, sure," Josie muttered.

Amanda stepped into the mirror.

"Don't leave me!" she cried. But her voice already sounded distant and faint, as though she were drowning and uttering the words through water. She didn't know if the other girls could even hear her now. She did not want to let go of Josie's hand— not for the life of herself.

Yet, ever so slowly, she let her fingers slip away from Josie's, and she vanished into the mirror.

The moment that Amanda was no longer holding on to Josie's hand, she found herself immersed in another world. Everything around her was a brilliant white, but as her eyes adjusted, she realized that it was moonlight streaming through the small diamond-shaped windows of the attic. It appeared that she had arrived at the same place she'd just left.

Only she was now alone.

Suddenly, agonizing screams tore through the air around her.

Amanda panicked and turned to step through the mirror and return to her friends in the attic, but she was stopped by the hard, impenetrable glass. Amanda felt along the mahogany edges and pounded on the veneer back, but there was no way she could retreat through the mirror. Faintly, from the other side, she heard Roxanne screaming, "Where are you, Amanda? Come back! Please!"

But Amanda Tucker was trapped.

III.

Amanda frantically called back to her friends, but it seemed that they could not hear her.

On the other side of the mirror, Roxanne exclaimed, "Josie, we've *got* to get Amanda's parents."

"What are we going to say to them? That their daughter vanished through a mirror?"

"I don't know."

Amanda could hear this conversation, and she called out again and again. But her voice did not seem to carry back the other way. Then she heard her sister speak up.

"I'll go get my sister. I'm not afraid," Sally declared.

"Don't!" Amanda shouted back, although it was now clear they couldn't hear her through the mirror.

"I know what," Josie went on. "You get your mother, Sally, while Roxanne goes through the mirror to find Amanda."

"Me?" Roxanne cried. "Why me?"

"Because..." there was a long pause, "...you're shorter than me. And I've got to be here to explain everything to Amanda's parents."

"I've got a better idea," Roxanne said. "*You* climb inside the mirror and look around, since this was your big idea for Amanda to go all the way in there."

"Okay," Josie said. "I'll grab Amanda and pull her back. But hold on to me. No matter what, don't let go of me."

Amanda heard a shuffling, but didn't see anyone, maybe because Josie was still hanging onto Roxanne. The mirror vibrated, followed by a loud *clunk*, then Josie and Roxanne broke into the light and tumbled onto the floor.

Amanda gasped. "Why on earth did you *both* come in here?"

"Roxanne wouldn't let go," Josie grumbled.

"You're darn tootin' I wouldn't let go," Roxanne declared, "because you told me not to."

Josie shrugged. "But I couldn't see anything." She turned to Amanda and explained, "So I guess I kind of yanked her inside with me."

"So let's turn right around and get out of here!" Roxanne exclaimed.

Amanda swallowed. "I don't think we can."

Roxanne gasped, "What?"

"I tried and couldn't go back through the mirror," Amanda said. "You couldn't even hear me shouting back to you."

Roxanne looked stricken.

"Nothing to worry about," Josie said. "I told Sally to get Amanda's parents. They'll know what to do."

No sooner had the words tumbled out of her mouth than the little spitfire cannonballed through the mirror.

"Why did you do that?" Amanda snapped.

Sally pouted, "You left me all alone and I got scared."

Despite her terror, Amanda grumbled, "You were supposed

to tell Mom and Dad."

"But I wanted to see what you guys were up to," Sally complained. "You always leave me behind, Amanda. I wasn't gonna let you ditch me, not again."

"I wish I'd never come here tonight," Roxanne sighed. "No offense, Amanda, but this is turning into the worst sleepover ever."

"Maybe Tulip will warn your parents," Josie suggested.

Amanda slumped. "Not that old dog. All she ever does is overeat and oversleep. She's so fat and lazy that she makes Garfield look like a hyper-active cat."

"But I saw this TV show about dogs," Josie said. "They have special instincts—like a sixth sense."

Although Sally never liked to agree with her sister, she shook her head. "Not Tulip. Our dad says she's the Queen of Canines."

"But she *was* trying to warn us," Roxanne cried hopefully. "I'm sure she'll get help, just like Lassie would."

A moment later, there was a *plop*, like fifty pounds of lard smacking the floor, and there squatted Her Highness the Hound. With considerable effort, the grizzled old beagle pushed herself to her stubby legs, waddled over to the girls, flopped down again, and gazed soulfully up them.

Josie cocked an eye at Roxanne. "Just like Lassie?"

The girls peered at each other, then looked nervously around the room in which they found themselves stuck. Without anyone saying a word, Amanda knew that her sister and Roxanne were recalling that terrifying night last summer on Shadow Island. It had been so out of character when the Tuckers' potbellied little dog had mobilized herself and accompanied the girls on what turned out to be a harrowing night. And now she seemed to be doing it again.

In a whisper, Amanda observed, "This is all so strange."

The girls had materialized in the same attic, except that the old, dark rafters and floorboards now gleamed brightly in the moonlight. Light-colored, almost blond, the lumber had the aroma of new wood.

Stored up here were leather-strapped trunks, embroidered carpet bags, suitcases, hatboxes, stacks of books, and an antique birdcage, except that the attic appeared to be brand-spanking new.

Amanda picked up a book lying within reach, *The Prince and the Pauper*. She opened it slowly. Inside the front cover it was inscribed: "To my dear Katie on the occasion of her 13th birthday, May 28, 1907. Father."

"What is going on here?" Josie asked. "This is too weird for words. It's like we went through the mirror, but we ended up in the exact same place."

"We did," Amanda stammered. "Except I...I think we've gone back in time."

Josie laughed. "Get real, Amanda."

"Look at the rafters and floor. They're almost new wood," Amanda pointed out. "And the attic is now finished, remember?"

"That is strange," Josie admitted.

"And look at this book," Roxanne said. "This edition was published in 1907. It's not new, but it looks like it's only a few years old. So," she paused, "it's like we went back to 1910 or 1912 or something."

"And look at the mirror!" Amanda gasped. "It's here, almost in the same spot, but it's not an antique. It looks brand new, too."

"Then why would it be stored up here?" Josie mused.

The girls turned back to the mirror, as if it might offer some clue that anything made sense here.

"Maybe it's a coincidence," Sally suggested.

"Or maybe not," Amanda reflected. "Maybe it's destiny. You know, something that was meant to be."

Josie snorted. "Get real, Amanda."

"We've got to find a way back!" Roxanne pleaded. "Now!"

"What's the hurry?" Josie said. "You know, this is all so creepy…and curious. Let's look around."

Roxanne was again wringing her hands. "I know something awful is going to happen to us if we don't get out of here."

Amanda didn't have the heart to remind her timid friend that they couldn't return through the mirror. Unless this was all a dream—or nightmare—they were trapped back in the early years of the twentieth century.

Her stomach churning, she wondered why the mirror had allowed them to journey back in time, but not to return to the present. It was such a mystery. What was the cause of it all? The mirror? Or the house?

Amanda recalled her dad's friend Bill Reilly saying that the house had been built sometime after the Spanish-American War of 1898. After the purchase, Mr. Reilly and her father had done a little research on the house. There was no record of the builder or the exact year when the house was completed. But, according to old city directories in a backroom of the Maysville Library, a family was listed at that address in 1902. Amanda couldn't remember their name, but they were likely the first people to live in the house.

Meanwhile, Sally was exploring the attic. She had opened a round hatbox and was trying on a salmon-colored hat with huge ostrich feathers. Standing there in her long purple gown from playing dress-up on the other side of the mirror, she was now quite a sight to behold. Sarah was such a dolled-up sight that Amanda and Josie couldn't help chuckling.

Roxanne squirmed. "Come on, you guys! This is no laughing matter. I want out of here."

"Just how do you suggest we get out of here?" Josie pressed.

Roxanne flapped her arms and pointed. "Through the mirror!"

"We can't," Amanda confessed. "I already tried."

"Then what are we going to do?" Roxanne asked in a panic.

The girls all fell silent. No one had a clue.

Amanda finally spoke up, trying to sound braver than she felt. "We've got to figure out why we've gone back in time. It's so strange to be in our own neighborhood, but more than a hundred years ago."

"Hey, look at these newspapers," Josie said, indicating a stack near one of the trunks.

Amanda rummaged through several of the papers. "They're the same as ours, the *Maysville Tribune and Gazette*. But they're all dated 1912!"

"But they almost look new," Roxanne gasped.

The girls began to sift through the newspapers, scanning the front pages.

"They're all in order, nice and tidy," Roxanne said, with a hint of satisfaction. "January 1st, the Republic of China is established."

Josie snorted. "And they're still trying to form a modern democracy."

"Look at this," Sally said. "January 6th, New Mexico becomes 47th state!"

"And January 9th, Textile Strike in Lawrence, Massachusetts," Amanda pointed out. "I studied that—it was the first time that women workers went on strike. It became known as the Bread and Roses Strike, supposedly because some of the women carried signs that read, 'We want bread, but roses, too.'"

"Here's another—on January 17th, Robert Scott expedition reaches South Pole, a month after Amundsen," Josie continued, in awe. "I've heard about those guys, too."

"It's like reading about history as it happened," Amanda said. "Amazing."

The girls quickly became absorbed in reading the headlines and outdoing each other with their own discoveries.

Sally found another article and announced, "On February 14th, Arizona became the 48th state!"

"Here's one from March 12th. Juliette Gordon Low forms the Girl Guides," Amanda said. "I think they became the Girl Scouts."

"Here's some big news," Josie declared. "On March 15th, pitcher Cy Young retired from baseball with 511 wins. Now that's history. He was the greatest."

Sally exclaimed, "On March 23rd the Dixie Cup was invented!"

Amanda and Roxanne chuckled. But, gripping a newspaper with two hands, Roxanne had become very quiet.

"Uh, guys," she finally whispered. "Maybe you heard what happened on April 15th of 1912."

The other girls gathered around Roxanne, reading silently the news bulletin.

TITANIC SINKS FOUR HOURS AFTER HITTING ICE-
BERG; 866 RESCUED BY CARPATHIA, PROBABLY 1,250
PERISH; ISMAY SAFE, MRS. ASTOR MAYBE, NOTED
NAMES MISSING

BIGGEST LINER PLUNGES TO THE BOTTOM AT 2:20
A.M. RESCUERS THERE TOO LATE

EXPECT TO PICK UP THE FEW HUNDREDS WHO TOOK
TO THE LIFEBOATS.

WOMEN AND CHILDREN FIRST

CUNARDER CARPATHIA RUSHING TO NEW YORK
WITH THE SURVIVORS.

SEA SEARCH FOR OTHERS

THE CALIFORNIA STANDS BY ON CHANCE OF PICKING
UP OTHER BOATS OR RAFTS.

OLYMPIC SENDS THE NEWS

ONLY SHIP TO FLASH WIRELESS MESSAGES TO SHORE
AFTER THE DISASTER.

– SPECIAL TO THE NEW YORK TIMES

"Wow," Amanda said. "It almost feels as if it's happening now."

The girls became subdued and only chuckled a little when Sally declared, "The Beverly Hills Hotel opened on the first of May!"

Josie perked up with news stories about baseball great Ty

Cobb and the legendary boxer Jack Johnson. And Amanda was excited to learn that the Bull Moose Party had nominated Theodore Roosevelt as its Presidential candidate in early August.

"You know he spoke here at Ellsworth Park in Maysville," Amanda said. "I bet it was during that 1912 campaign. And he was shot right before a speech in Milwaukee. He still went on stage, opened his coat to show everyone his bloodstained shirt, and declared it takes more than that to kill a bull moose. People said the thick speech in his vest pocket slowed the bullet and kept it from going into his heart. And even though he'd been shot, Teddy apologized for not making a long speech, and still spoke for quite a while—with the bullet in him!"

"My kind of guy," Josie said. "Except there's no news about it here."

"It must have happened later that year," Amanda said.

But then they came to the bottom of the stack. "Which means we must be here in mid-August. Maybe even the same date as in our present time," Amanda said.

"Unless they have another pile of more recent newspapers somewhere else," Josie said.

The girls turned their attention to the interior of the attic.

Peeking through the small diamond window in one of the gables at the front of the house, Amanda recognized the globes of the street lamps and the brick sidewalks that lined both sides of Elm Street and wound through the park across the street.

"It is all so familiar," she muttered. "But at the same time so different."

"Same time, Amanda?" Josie said. "Ha, ha. That's funny."

"Not really," Roxanne complained.

Although the street lamps had not changed, many of the trees in the neighborhood and park looked small. But a large number were towering in height. They must be Dutch elms, Amanda realized. Her dad had told her that some disease had swept across the country about fifty years ago and killed all the elms in every town across America, including throughout Maysville.

Amanda recognized a few other ancients, notably the pair of towering English oaks near the pavilion in the park. The magnificent trees didn't look any smaller than in the present day. But then again, at the turn of the last century, those trees were already more than two hundred years old. However, the two sycamores in Amanda's front yard, huge in the present time, were now saplings, as were so many of the trees in the park.

Amanda gasped. "Hey, you guys, look!"

The three other girls crowded around the window.

"You know that old shagbark hickory tree in the park that was struck by lightning last year?" Amanda said. "Well, there it is!"

"It's just a skinny little thing!" Josie exclaimed.

Prior to the lightning strike, the tree had anchored the northeast corner of the park.

Squeezed together by the small window, the girls looked up and down the brick streets in front of the house and around the city park.

Amanda recognized most of the Victorian houses that graced the street, although they were now truly "painted ladies." Each house was decorated in amazing bright colors—greens, purples, and blues. The festive, whimsical painting was much different from the staid whites and grays Amanda was used to seeing in the neighborhood.

Here and there an empty lot interrupted the sweep of elegant houses.

"Look!" Roxanne said. "That's going to be my house!"

Down the block they could see the foundation and frame going up on what would become one of the finest houses on the street.

"The neighborhood looks so eerie," Amanda observed. "It's like a blend of the old and the new."

"What are those?" Sally asked, pointing to the curb.

"Hitching posts," Josie said. "We're back in horse and buggy days!"

For a moment, the girls looked at the posts in front of all the houses on the brick street. Like the one in front of Amanda's house, most were cast-iron horse heads, each with a brass ring like a bit in its mouth.

Other posts featured a globe on top with a ring through it or two rings on the side. And a few were cast-iron jockeys, each with a ring in an extended right hand.

"They show black people as servants," Amanda explained. "But in the old days, some of those black jockeys may actually have been markers on the Underground Railroad. If a green ribbon was tied on the statue's arms, it meant that it was a safe house. It's kind of ironic, if you think about."

"Wow, Amanda. You're a walking encyclopedia," Josie kidded.

Amanda shrugged. "I've always loved history. Not the war and politics stuff, but how everyday people lived."

Not to be outdone, Josie pointed out, "It was actually the end of horse-and-buggy days back then. People were also driving the first cars, like the Oldsmobile Gas Buggy. Of course, Oldsmobile had already merged with Buick to become General Motors, and there was Henry Ford and Model T. There were well-known cars like Cadillacs, and cars nobody remembers today, like the Peerless and the Mercer Raceabout, which was a really cool sports car." She noticed the other girls staring at her.

"Hey," Josie explained. "So Amanda loves history. And I love cars."

Amanda nodded. "You're a car nut, we all know that."

"And I'm going to design cars—the cars of the *future,*" Josie emphasized.

Before she got carried away, the girls returned their attention to the small window.

Across the way, the pavilion in the park was the same elegant limestone, minus the graffiti and cigarette butts that were the legacy of the high school kids who now hung out there at lunch time and occasionally late in the evening.

"Look!" Amanda exclaimed. "The fountain is working!"

"Lemme see!" Sally cried, straining on tiptoes to peek through the window.

Through the tree branches they gazed at the three streams of water arcing from the mouths of a bouquet of fish, carved from stone, from the very center of the pond. There were lily pads with white blossoms and Amanda occasionally caught glimpses of goldfish as they surfaced, their radiant orange flashing in the soft light from the street lamps and the full moon.

To Amanda, their neighborhood seemed to be an even more charming place than she had ever imagined.

"Look at that!" Sally squealed as a horse pulling a black buggy clip-clopped down the brick street right past them.

Moments later, a black car, with its engine clicking like a sewing machine, putted by from the opposite direction.

"Model T," Josie stated in an authoritative tone.

Amanda sighed, "It must have been so wonderful living back at this time."

"What do you mean?" Josie said. "We *are* living back then."

"I want to go home!" Roxanne said. "Now! This is more than weird—it's scary."

"Come on!" Josie urged. "How often have you ever had a chance to travel back in time?"

Indeed, Amanda had often wondered, especially after moving to their new home, what life had been like in Maysville in those days when the lovely town was growing and the beautiful Victorian houses were being built.

At least nothing bad had happened to them, although they seemed stuck back in the year 1912. Even Tulip didn't appear overly concerned. The old dog had sniffed around the attic for a moment. Then, sighing with boredom, she'd waddled over to the far corner, turned around three times, settled into a mess of old clothes, and promptly dozed off.

But Amanda could not forget the strange noises...and the screams she'd heard when she'd first tumbled through the magical mirror. And what about the warning of the old man that the mirror was cursed? Even if it was a little thrilling to see her town as it was a hundred years earlier, they needed to get out of there.

"Uh, everybody," Amanda said, "maybe we should try the mirror again."

"Yes!" Roxanne exclaimed. "Let's get out of here now!"

Amanda muttered, "Just don't get your hopes up."

Sally's mouth dropped open. "What do you mean 'try' the mirror? We can't go back?"

Amanda looked at her kid sister, who crept over to the mirror and pressed her hand against the hard and unyielding mahogany veneer of the back. "It won't work," Sally exclaimed.

Roxanne and Josie stepped up and also pushed against the back of the mirror, but it was impenetrable.

"How's the front?" Josie suggested. But the silvery glass of the mirror proved to be as solid as the back.

Roxanne exclaimed, "We really are *trapped!*"

A deep fear engulfed the four girls.

Sally tried to hold back tears. "Does this mean we'll have to spend the rest of our lives here?"

"If we're not killed first," Roxanne exclaimed.

Amanda shushed her, with a quick nod in her sister's direction. "But Mom and Dad will look for us, Sally!"

"Not until morning," Josie observed.

"And they'll never figure out we went through the mirror," Roxanne pointed out. "Like Alice in *Through the Looking Glass.*"

"And it's not safe here!" Roxanne cried.

"How do you know?" Josie demanded. "Nothing bad has happened to us. It's kind of cool."

Amanda added, "Everything is so old-fashioned and interesting here—and comfortable too. Look at Tulip! She's snoozing away."

The girls glanced at the old dog. Sunk in a deep slumber, she made little whiffing sounds as if she were enjoying the sweetest of dreams.

"That dog is just clueless," Roxanne mourned. "We're going to get killed."

"We can tell people who we are and how we came to be here," Josie said brightly. "They'll help us get back to the present."

"Who will believe us?" Roxanne groaned. "They'll think we're crazy."

"We'll figure out how get back to our own time," Amanda insisted. "In the meantime we can learn firsthand about how people lived at the turn of the century. We'll be *living* history. It'll be fun."

No sooner were the words out of her mouth than a blood-curdling scream pierced the black of that summer night.

"What was that?" Sally cried, her brown eyes flashing with terror.

"I don't know," Roxanne breathed. "But whatever it is, that creature is not human."

IV.

Another long, anguished scream pierced the calm of that summer night.

Wrenched from her slumber, Tulip snapped awake, trembled, and dove under the pile of old clothes on which she had been snoozing. The girls shivered, too, as they crept to the back of the attic and peered through one of the diamond-shaped windows that overlooked the backyard.

The Victorian garden below was filled with a profusion of begonias, snapdragons, and other flowers. There were lawn ornaments too—a birdbath, sundial, gazing balls, cast-iron benches, and urns overflowing with blossoms. Amanda's heart ached when she recalled just hours ago seeing her mother, with a scarf on her head and cloth gloves on her hands, as she weeded those same flowerbeds, except a hundred years later.

Toward the back of the yard were a few small, wood buildings: garden shed, outhouse, root cellar, dovecote, and another shed with a stovepipe—maybe a smokehouse. Along the east side of the lot stood a carriage house and small stable, which had become the Tuckers' garage.

Except for those terrible screams, everything now appeared tranquil. Yet in the quiet of that night and the pale light of a full moon rising, the atmosphere of the yard felt ominous.

There was muttering in the air, just as Amanda had heard during her first nights living in the house. Then another shriek tore through the still air—another high-pitched scream.

It was coming from the other side of some high bushes that bordered the backyard and the driveway in front of the carriage house. Amanda glanced that way and saw a sleek black horse rearing high on its hind legs.

"Over there!" she whispered, pointing toward the carriage house. Deep in the shadows of the shrubs, a man was thrashing the horse with a riding whip.

Dressed in a black suit, tie and hat, he looked like a gentleman. But he raised the short whip and savagely brought it down again, and yet again. Tied to a hitching post, the lathered horse could not escape the lashes. Eyes rolling in its head, it veered away from each blow, screaming in that high pitch that clearly was not human.

"We've got to stop him!" Josie cried out. "He's beating that poor horse to death."

"How?" Amanda asked helplessly. "We're from another time. Look at how we're dressed."

Glancing at themselves, the girls realized that, just moments ago, they had been posing as fashion models in clunky high heels, gaudy clothes, and big hats, with gauzy scarves wrapped their necks. And they were still dressed in those outlandish clothes!

"We'd never be able to explain ourselves," Josie groaned.

"We can say we're from France," Roxanne suggested.

Amanda rolled her eyes.

"We have to stop him!" Sally urged.

"You're darn tootin'," Josie agreed and started toward the door, just as the black-suited man swung the whip again.

Then, to their surprise and horror, the girls realized that he was *not* striking the horse. He was thrashing a young man crouched in the doorway of the carriage house, and the terrified horse was actually trying to get away from the crazed man.

Through the leafy bushes and branches, and the rearing horse, the girls caught snatches of the scene. The boy was dressed in a blue workshirt and pants of a rough fabric held up by broad suspenders. He had shock of gleaming blond hair and a face with prominent nose and high cheekbones.

"Amanda!" Josie gasped. "That's John Brandowski. What's he doing back here in past?"

"Who knows? Why are *we* here?" Roxanne whispered.

"That's not him," Amanda said slowly. "He has the same face, almost, but that guy is older. He must be at least seventeen."

"But he looks just like John," Roxanne exclaimed.

"Yeah, he's the spitting image of your *boyfriend,*" Josie said.

"He is *not* my boyfriend," Amanda sputtered, out of principle. But she was too shocked to argue. This young man did strikingly resemble her classmate—a good-looking guy who she did want to be her boyfriend. He not only had John's face—those high cheekbones and floppy blond hair, what she called his "chicken noodle soup hair"—but also his lean and muscular body.

Normally, the other girls would have gone on kidding Amanda about her crush on John Brandowski, but it was a terrible scene they were witnessing below.

Roxanne gasped, "Whoever he is, we've got to help that poor

boy, before that sicko kills him."

Why doesn't that broad-shouldered boy defend himself, Amanda wondered. Just then, the man in the black suit lowered his hand. Catching his breath, he glared at the boy. "How dare you sneak into my home in the dead of night!" he roared. "Let this be a lesson. I do not want to ever see you here again. Now get off my property, you sorry mongrel! You're nothing but a Pole! A low-class immigrant!"

Once more, the man brought the whip down on the blond boy. Amanda winced. But this time, quick as light, the young man rose to his full height and snatched the whip away.

The man in the black suit was instantly transformed from cruel bully to groveling coward. "Don't you dare strike me!" he whined.

The youth raised the whip.

"Don't hurt me," the older man whimpered, falling to his knees. "I beseech you. Please don't hit me."

In a deep, yet melodious voice, the young man answered, carefully picking the words, as though they were new to him, "I would never lower myself."

He snapped the whip in his bare hands as though it were a twig, flung it onto the ground, and whirled away.

In the light of the rising moon, Amanda could see that the young man's blond hair lay flat on his head, and his blue eyes were set wide and deep in this face. She also noticed a red slash from the whip across his left cheek.

Regaining his courage, the man in black scrambled to his feet and called after the boy, "That's right, you'd better hightail it out of here! And don't come back! I forbid you to see my daughter ever again."

The young man paused just long enough to glance back at the man in black who sprang back and blubbered, "Please don't hurt me!"

Shaking his head, the young man declared in a sorrowful tone, "I am leaving."

"And you'll be leaving Maysville altogether," the man warned as the youth turned away, "or I'll have the law after you. You're trespassing! I'm ringing up the constable on my new *telly*-phone! I will have you deported back to the squalor of your old country or sent to prison, where you'll rot in a filthy cell for the rest of your life."

Without another word, the young man strode down the lane along the east side of the house. As he faded into the night, the older man pulled off his hat and turned his pallid face toward the house. Amanda noticed that he parted his hair down the middle and sported a waxy, black, handlebar mustache.

Suddenly, the screen-door below the girls slapped shut, and a hefty, middle-aged woman in ankle-length dress and flouncy white petticoat waddled out along the walk to the carriage house. Her hair drawn back in a bun, she exclaimed, "Is that boy finally gone, Clement?"

"The coward ran into the night," the man gloated, "after I broke my horsewhip over his back."

"Gone for good?" she asked.

"Good riddance to bad rubbish."

"But I just heard noises up in the attic! I fear there's someone else up there!"

"Egad!" the man cried. "Must be accomplices of the boy, trying to help him kidnap our dear Katie. I tell you, Mabel, I've had enough of these immigrants. They're vermin, no better than rats and cockroaches. These intruders must have snuck in the front door while I was busy thrashing the boy out here. What has the world come to when a man can't sleep peacefully in his own home? Fetch my shotgun, woman. And then ring up the constable!"

"What are you going to do, Clement?" the woman asked.

"Blast them to kingdom come!" the man yelled. "They've broken into my home. I have every right to defend my property and shoot them dead. Now, hurry while the rats are trapped in the attic."

"We've got to get out of here!" Amanda exclaimed, as if any of the girls clustered at the attic window needed prompting.

As they made for the door, the girls realized that they could only wobble along in the high-heels, so they kicked off the shoes, which clattered into a corner of the attic. Scampering on bare feet, they padded down the stairs.

As they swept past the rear bedroom, Amanda noticed a girl sitting at a vanity and crying bitterly.

But that's *my* room, she thought, stopping short, astonished. Except that, peeking into the room, Amanda could see a wash jug and bowl on a table, a brass bed, and a flowery cross-stitch framed and mounted on the wall about the fireplace: *Home is Where the Heart Is.*

Reaching out her arms to Amanda, the young woman begged, "Help me! I can't live without Jan. We hope to be married. Do not run away! Are you not his loyal friends? Please help me get out of here!"

"*Yon?*" Josie muttered, behind Amanda. "What kind of name is that?"

"Yes, Jan. He is the love of my life. And my name is Katie," the young woman declared. "Don't you know him? Aren't you going to help us?"

In a quick breath, Amanda explained, "*Jan* must be a Polish name. Like *John*. It's the same name as my great-grandfather."

To the girls' dismay, they heard someone heavily clumping up the stairs. "I'll shoot you dead!" a man's voice roared. "Prepare to meet your Maker!"

Amanda hated to abandon the young woman, but they had to get out of that house—fast. "Run!" she cried, and the girls fled for their lives.

It's so strange that Sally and I have to escape from our own house where we should have been safe, she thought. More bewildered and frightened than ever, the girls rushed to the far end of the hall.

"What's going on here?" Clement shouted up the stairs. "Katie Blackburn! Are you conspiring with those vile immigrants—after I forbade you to have any contact with them?"

Luckily, Amanda and Sally knew the layout of the house, since they'd explored every nook and cranny after moving there. As the man rounded the newel post on the second floor, shotgun in hand, the girls eased into the shadows and crept down the narrow backstairs that led to the kitchen. They peeked around the corner of the pantry, lined with jars of jellies and jams, and into the room.

No one appeared to be there, so they carefully tiptoed past a large white-enameled stove, with legs and knobby handles to operate the gas jets, and the icebox.

"Oh no! What about Tulip?" Sally whispered.

The girls looked around, but the little dog was nowhere in sight.

Amanda knew they could not go back upstairs. "Tulip has this way of looking out for herself...and only herself. She'll be okay."

"No, she won't," Sally scowled.

Amanda hated to abandon their pudgy little dog, but at that moment they had no choice. "We have to get out of here, Sally, *now!*"

Josie paused. "Wow! Get a load of these rooms."

"Come on," Amanda groaned. "We don't have time."

But the girls couldn't help glancing into the dining room and the parlor.

Persian and Oriental carpets adorned the hardwood floors in both rooms. Elegant chairs, table, and large hutch dominated the dining room, while the parlor was crammed with furniture—over-stuffed horsehair chairs with carved frames of vines, leaves, and acorns, and dark cherry-wood tables with marble tops. There were dried flowers in vases, statuettes, and knick-knacks everywhere, along with a stereograph and photographs mounted in pairs on stiff cards. The parlor had a few lamps with Tiffany stained-glass shades, and other lamps of painted china and brass, the shades decorated with fringe, bows, and rosettes. Overhead hung a candelabra with gaslights. A Currier and Ives lithograph hung over the stone fireplace.

"Hurry!" Amanda whispered.

Roxanne in the lead, they cut across the parlor and paused in the foyer next to a hollowed elephant leg. It was filled with umbrellas and walking sticks. There was also a little table with a few letters and postcards. Amanda noticed the morning edition of the *Maysville Tribune and Gazette* newspaper. It was dated August 25, 1912!

"Just like the papers in the attic," Sally said.

The four girls were frozen in awe. Indeed, they had gone back in time more than a hundred years ago.

"What now?" Josie asked.

Amanda was startled from her state of disbelief. "Outside!"

"Then what?" Roxanne asked.

"I don't know,"Amanda said. "We just need to get away from the house."

The girls had lingered a moment too long. A boy in knickers and Buster Brown shoes whirled around the corner from the back hallway and into the parlor. "There they are, Papa!" he squealed. "I found them!"

The stout woman lumbered into the room, a small but evil-looking ax clenched in her hands. "Help!" she caterwauled. "They're here!"

"By the door!" the boy screamed. "They're gypsies, Father!"

The man named Clement raced into view. "Stop this instant!" he shouted, raising a shotgun. As the girls screamed and rushed out the front door, a blast rattled the windows and plaster exploded from the wall right where they had been standing.

As she dashed out onto the porch, the last of the four girls, Amanda glanced back at the ragged hole in the foyer wall, the plaster shattered. So that was the mysterious patch of repaired plaster that Mr. Reilly had discussed with her father.

The girls sped down the front walk as another blast whizzed past them, just over their heads, and shredded the bushes that fringed the west edge of the yard.

Sprinting across the brick street to Ellsworth Park, they slipped into a clump of lilac bushes in the northeast corner. They hid there, quivering with fear, and glanced back to the house. Shotgun clasped in his hands, the man in black prowled on the front porch.

"That man tried to kill us," Roxanne gasped.

"And he missed, at close range," Josie snorted. "He must be cross-eyed."

"It's not funny!" Roxanne said.

"Who's joking?" Josie answered. "I'm too young and good-looking to die. Especially," she added, "a hundred years before I was born."

From their hiding place, the girls caught their breath and tried to calm their nerves. But Roxanne and Sally looked like wide-eyed zombies, and Amanda's heart was pounding in her chest. None of them could say anything, except Josie who grumbled, "I'd like to bend that shotgun over that jerk's head." Despite her bravado, however, she too appeared to be terrified.

Luckily, the man had not pursued them across the street. He just paced back and forth like a caged animal on the porch.

There were a few people on the street, out for an evening stroll. It must be late, Amanda thought, but back then it must have been safe to be out well after dark. None of them looked alarmed. If any had heard the shotgun blasts, they might have thought that a Model T had backfired on a nearby street.

They could stop someone and ask for help, but the four girls were barefoot and decked out in the wild dress-up clothes. Amanda was sure no one would believe their story about how they'd traveled back in time.

Down the street, a young couple was pushing a buggy, probably trying to get their baby to fall asleep. Glancing over her shoulder, Amanda also noticed an old man in a tweed suit strolling toward the corner. Then, another man pedaled down the brick street on a bicycle with a huge front wheel. He paused in front of the house—their house—and braced himself with his left foot on the hitching post.

"What's the commotion, good sir?" the man asked from his high perch.

Clement hesitated a moment and then exclaimed, "Gypsies—gypsy thieves! Yes, indeed, Simon. My wife caught them trying to rob our house. They were dressed in strange clothes, and they tried to murder us in our sleep! I'm standing guard in case they double back."

"Gypsies, you say?"

"Yes! Perhaps you should go after them!"

The man perched on the two-wheel cycle shook his head.

"You're not a coward, are you, Simon Walters!" the man on the porch sneered.

"But it's after dark, Judge Blackburn. And I'm not armed."

The judge sighed. "I suppose that it would be prudent to wait for the constable. My good wife has called him on the *telly*-phone."

Simon Walters gasped. "You have one of those devices?"

Judge Blackburn stood proud. "One must keep up with the times."

"To think—talking through a wire. What will folks come up with next?" Simon responded. "I myself don't trust those contraptions."

"Why, my man, they're handy when one is in need of protection. And those gypsies are a menace to the community. We'll need to raise a posse, or they'll rob us as we sleep in our beds, as sure as you were born!" The judge glanced toward the park and shouted into the night. "Hear this, gypsy thieves! The constable will soon be after you. We'll hunt you down and lock you up, or more likely we'll shoot you dead in your tracks!"

"You say they're hiding over there?" Simon asked. On his bicycle he made a slow loop in the street and scanned the park. "Indeed, Judge. Look over there. I saw those bushes flutter a bit."

Judge Blackburn shouldered the shotgun.

"Get down!" Amanda said, shoving her sister and friends flat on the ground under the lilacs, just as the judge pulled the trigger. Twin blasts of the shotgun tore through the leaves and splintered small branches, the pellets whizzing over their heads.

"That was close," Josie gasped as the echo of the blast rumbled through the neighborhood. "That man is crazy."

A light went on in the window of one house across the street, and then another.

Keeping low, the girls crawled backward through the bushes. They retreated to another clump farther from the house, and then slipped away, putting some distance between themselves and the houses that lined Elm Street.

They hurried along a brick sidewalk that wound through the park.

"We'll have to find a good hiding place," Amanda exclaimed.

"And get back to our own time," Roxanne said.

For once, Josie had no further suggestions, and Sally was too frightened to speak.

Luckily, the geography of the park was similar to that of their own time so they knew of several hiding places, mostly clumps of bushes that dotted the landscape. The four girls slipped into the middle of the park and huddled in a thicket just west of the fountain and goldfish pond.

"We can't stay here," Roxanne moaned, wringing her hands. "They're sure to search the park and find us. We need to get farther away."

"But where?" Amanda said.

No one had an answer.

"I don't know why we've ended up in the past," Amanda went on. "But I'm sure there's only one way back—through that mirror. So we can't wander too far away from the house, since we're going to have to sneak back in there."

Roxanne nearly collapsed. "What? Are you crazy, Amanda?"

"Do you have a better idea?" Josie asked.

"I just want to go home," Roxanne said, her lower lip trembling a little.

Staring into the distance, Sally whispered, "Look. There's a man on a horse."

The man was a police officer with a crisply brimmed hat and dark blue uniform. He was mounted on a chestnut horse that clip-clopped over the brick pavement of Elm Street. In his left hand, he lightly held the reins. And in his right hand he gripped a rifle, propped on his thigh, the steel barrel angled toward the sky.

In the moonlight and quiet of the night, the girls could easily see the men and hear most of their conversation, even across the open spaces of the park. The judge was not a soft-spoken man. And the others responded in kind, speaking loudly, sure that the "gypsy thieves" were long gone.

Judge Blackburn bellowed to the officer, "Gypsy thieves, Calhoun! Breaking into my house!"

The man with the bicycle called out, "I expect they're halfway to Bloomington by now, Constable."

"The last thing we need in this town is gypsies, Simon," the constable responded.

"Old Judge Blackburn put a scare into them," Simon chortled. "Sent a blast right at them. They shot out of those bushes like cottontail rabbits."

The constable snorted. "I haven't heard of any gypsies camping around here lately, but I'll keep a lookout."

"You know, they may be immigrant agitators," Simon speculated.

There was silence for a moment. Then the constable responded, "There have been a few immigrants riling up the workers at the zinc foundry and brickyard, telling them they need a union. Now they're stirring up trouble in our peaceful neighborhoods. It's an outrage."

"I've read about those people," Simon responded. "They're Communists."

"I'm deputizing both of you men on the spot," the constable replied. "We'll get together a bunch of the boys to search the park and spread out from there. I suspect that they'll try to slink back across the railroad tracks to their side of town. So if we don't catch 'em around here, we'll go down to the Bottoms and smoke 'em out."

"That could be dangerous, Amos," Simon answered.

The constable nodded. "We'll be fully armed. We'll shoot first and ask questions later. You coming, Judge?"

Judge Blackburn replied in his loud voice, "I'd surely love to blast them, Constable Calhoun. Even a pack of females. But I'd better stand guard here and protect my home in case they sneak back."

"That makes sense, sir," the constable said. "Simon and I

will head back to the station and raise the alarm."

"I had a good look at them, Calhoun, and I'm certain they're gypsies," Judge Blackburn grumbled. "They're barefoot and wearing crazy clothes—all bright colors and strange hats."

"We'll check everywhere, including the outskirts of town, where those gypsies usually camp," the constable said.

"When you catch them, Calhoun, I don't want to see them in my court," Judge Blackburn went on, "if you catch my drift. Either run them out of town forever—or better yet, shoot them dead."

Simon Walters gasped. "In cold blood?"

"A man has a right to protect his own home, and yours may be next," the judge contended. "It will be a lesson to any other vagrants who wander into our peaceful community."

Without another word Judge Blackburn strode back into the house, and the other two men, Simon Walters and Constable Calhoun, turned away, one on horseback and the other on the bicycle.

"That Judge Blackburn sure is a mean one," Simon remarked as they headed down Elm Street.

The constable chuckled. "Better not let him hear you say that, Simon, or he'll have you up on charges for something. But he's exactly what we need in this town. I will be pleased when he's elected mayor. I suspect that's why he doesn't want any bad press about any…uh…private family matters, if you know what I mean."

"But everyone knows that his daughter is running around with a common laborer, and an immigrant to boot," Simon pointed out.

From their hiding place near the goldfish pond, the girls saw the men turn right at the corner of Orchard Street. Amanda figured they were going downtown, to where the police station was located, as it was in the present day.

The girls watched in silence as the two men disappeared into the night.

"Whew," Roxanne sighed. "That was close."

"But they'll be back soon with a posse," Amanda pointed out.

"More like a mob," Josie said. "And they're wrong. We're not gypsies."

"Well, we are wearing these weird clothes," Sally said.

Amanda nodded. "When that snotty kid, who must be his son, called us gypsies it must have given the judge that idea. Seems he doesn't want a scandal about his daughter being in love with a Polish guy."

Roxanne sighed. "But we're not immigrants or gypsies."

"And we didn't do anything wrong," Sally squeaked.

"They caught us *in* their house," Josie pointed out. "That Judge Blackburn and his wife Mabel must have thought we were trying to rob them."

"But it's *our* house," Sally pointed out. "My sister and I live there."

"I know, but only in the present time," Amanda said. "No one would ever believe us, and they sure don't like outsiders."

"They'll never give us a chance to explain ourselves," Josie said. "They'll hunt us down and shoot us dead."

"Don't say that!" Roxanne exclaimed.

Josie shrugged. "At least those dopes don't know where we are right now. We need to figure out how to get back to the present."

"I've always been curious about how people in Maysville

lived in the past," Amanda reflected, "and so far I don't like it." She was actually horrified. "That Judge Blackburn is so cruel, and the constable isn't much better. We've got to find a way out of here. Unless we do, we'll be trapped here forever."

"Trapped?" Roxanne gasped. "Forever?"

"Yes!" Amanda insisted.

"Don't say that!" Roxanne cried. "My mom will kill me."

"If you don't get back, you'll never have to worry about that," Josie said. "Unless she finds a way to come back in time herself."

Amanda sighed. "The judge thinks we're friends of Jan Brandowski and are helping him elope with his daughter Kate. He wants us gone. Permanently, if you know what I mean."

"Dead?" Roxanne gulped.

"Yes, as in no living witnesses," Josie stated. "As in dead girls tell no tales."

Roxanne kneaded her hands together. "So what now?"

Amanda put a sober expression on her face. "We'll double-back to the judge's house. I mean, our house. I mean...." She fell silent. It was too much to comprehend.

Roxanne gasped, "Back to the house? Why?"

"To find a way back to our own time."

"How?"

"We can try the mirror again, but I have a feeling it won't let us go back to our time until we figure out what we have to do here. Here's what I think: we have to talk to that girl—what was her name? Katie?"

Amanda looked at the others. "She's at the heart of this mystery." She didn't say anything about all the crying and moaning that had been keeping her awake long into the nights. But Amanda felt sure it was part of the reason they had been brought through the mirror.

"Maybe if we help her," she continued, "we'll be able to go back through the mirror. Or at least find some clue about why we came back in time. Which might help us figure out how we can get back to the present."

"Shouldn't we wait until morning?" Roxanne asked. "When it's daylight?"

Josie snorted, "Right. You think if we walked around barefoot in these crazy dresses, skirts, blouses, scarves, and hats—nobody would notice us?"

Sally brightened. "Maybe we can just go to the present, our own time, when it gets to be morning!"

"Or maybe," Amanda groaned, "if we don't solve this mystery before the break of day…we'll be stuck here forever."

Josie's mouth dropped open. "That means we only have a few hours left."

"Don't say that," Roxanne moaned. "Please don't say that."

V.

As the girls hunkered down in the bushes, Josie said, "I'd *still* like to look around town, as long as we're stuck here. This experience is so cool."

Roxanne resolutely disagreed. "There is nothing *cool* about being hunted down."

Josie shrugged. "We can easily outwit those lame-brains. And when will we ever get another chance to actually *live* in the past?"

Amanda, too, had often wondered what her hometown had been like years ago. But still she also realized the grave danger of their situation. "Maybe if we can solve this mystery—why we were able to go back in time and what exactly is going on here—it will be safe enough for us to do a little exploring. Or maybe we can come back another time."

"You are both crazy," Roxanne cried. "*If* we ever get back home, I will *never* come back here. And please do me a favor, Amanda. Do not invite me to another sleepover, not ever again. In fact, I won't go anywhere near your house."

"I just want to go home," Sally moaned.

We are going to our house, Amanda thought, *but it sure feels strange to be so afraid of our own home.*

"Everyone seems to hate us because they think we're gypsies or immigrants," Roxanne pointed out.

"Just because we're different," Josie added.

Amanda sighed. "I always thought that the past was romantic, and everyone was nice and kind to each other."

"Turns out they're cruel. And trigger-happy," Roxanne observed. "Especially that horrible Judge Blackburn."

That sobered the girls, even Josie. "Maybe we should forget the sightseeing, and get the heck out of here."

Amanda nodded. She had invited them to the sleepover, at least Josie and Roxanne, even though she knew that something was wrong, that restless spirits were haunting their new home. And Sally might be a pest, but she was still her sister and needed her care and protection. Amanda felt it was up to her to somehow lead them safely home again.

"We've got sneak up into Katie's bedroom and talk with her *now*," she said. "It won't be long before Constable Calhoun gets his posse together, and they'll be hot on our trail."

Josie snorted. "Posse? More like a lynch mob."

Sally squirmed.

"Thanks a lot," Roxanne said. "So, if we don't get shot, we'll be strung up. But what about Judge Blackburn? He's there guarding the house with a shotgun."

"We can cut across the park to the corner of Orchard and Elm streets, then sneak down the alley and slip into the backyard," Amanda suggested.

However, no one appeared eager to leave their hiding place and return to the house.

"Come on," Amanda urged. "We're just sitting ducks here."

Reluctantly, the other girls nodded.

Although it was against her sisterly principles, Amanda grasped Sally's hand as the girls stole across the park, slipping from one bush to another. When they approached Orchard Street, they paused in a cluster of dogwood trees. "There aren't many people out," Amanda said. "When we get to the house next door to ours, we can slip into the bushes and around back."

"I thought these were the good old days, but lots of people sure don't like immigrants," Josie said.

"Hey, all of our grandparents or great-grandparents were immigrants, weren't they?" Amanda noted. "Remember the newspapers we saw in the attic and hallway? We're back in 1912. There are millions of immigrants, especially from Eastern and Southern Europe—including my great-grandparents—pouring into the country."

"My dad says when his grandparents came here from Lithuania," Josie said "they were treated like some sort of inferior kind of people. Almost like animals. Good if you needed work done, but otherwise, they weren't welcome."

"Same thing with my ancestors," Amanda said."

"My mom's Russian and Italian," Roxanne said. "And my dad's Irish and Swiss, and other stuff, too."

"People said the immigrants could never become Americans," Amanda went on. "But my dad says I'm as American as can be, because I'm Polish, German, Slovenian, Lithuanian, Italian—a blend of all sorts of things."

"Me too!" Sally piped, as though it were a coincidence.

Amanda glanced at her little sister. "Maybe because we have the same parents and grandparents."

"Oh yeah."

"Along with being Lithuanian, I'm Czech and Romanian—hey, maybe a little gypsy too," Josie said. "With Scotch-Irish thrown in. That's where I get my red hair and fighting spirit. At least that's what my mom says."

Amanda nodded. "My dad likes to joke that we're all a bunch of mutts, which are the best kind of dogs."

"You know, it's funny, but these bigoted people we've met, like the judge, are children of immigrants, too," Josie said. "Only their ancestors came here a little earlier."

Amanda glanced over to the fountain where the goldfish floated among the lily pads, and then around the neighborhood. "Everything is so pretty here," she observed. "But people are so intolerant—at least some of them. My dad says that when this neighborhood was being built up it was a pleasant time in American history, after the Spanish-American War and before World War I. But it seems like there's a lot simmering beneath the surface, like a pot that has a lid on it, and is about to boil over."

"Yeah, look how they treated people," Josie said. "You know, my great-grandparents, the ones from Lithuania, worked in the stockyards up in Chicago."

"My great-grandfather too, on my mom's side," Amanda said. "He was from Poland. Then he came down here when he heard they were hiring in the zinc foundry and the brickyard."

"Mine too," Josie said.

"My dad says there was discrimination against every immigrant group," Amanda recalled. "First, the English didn't like the Scotch-Irish and the Germans. Then everyone discriminated against the Irish. They even put up signs: N.I.N.A. That meant 'No Irish Need Apply.' And black people were treated worse...a lot worse."

"And what about Native Americans?" Roxanne added. "They were the first immigrants here."

"And Jewish people," Josie said. "Man, they were persecuted in Europe *and* in America."

Like her dad, Amanda loved American history and she had read stacks of books. She knew that many immigrants, mostly from countries in Eastern and Southern Europe, had come to work in Chicago.

"Did you ever read that book by Upton Sinclair?" Amanda said. "It's called *The Jungle.*"

Josie shook her head.

"It's about immigrants, mostly from Poland and Lithuania—like your great-grandparents—who worked in the meat-packing industry in Chicago," she explained. "It was such a cruel life—long hours for low wages—and so gross. If someone fell in a vat, they just fished out the bones and sold the stuff as Durham's pure lard."

"Yuck!" Josie exclaimed.

"A lot of those immigrants moved here to Maysville," Amanda went on, "to work in the factories, like in the zinc foundry, and in the coal mines, brickyards, and rail yards."

"Thanks for the history lesson," Josie said.

"It's *our* history," Amanda pointed out. "That's what history really is. It's about how people lived. And not just the rich and famous, but common people, too."

"And now we're living history all over again," Roxanne said.

Sally shook her head. "We're living history before it happened, at least for us."

"Weird," Josie said. "You know, to the people here, we're not even born yet."

"*Our parents* aren't even born yet," Roxanne pointed out.

Josie's mouth dropped open. "Wow."

"It's okay 'cause we're just visiting," Sally said. "Right, Amanda?"

"I hope so," Amanda said.

"So, is anyone else wondering—where's Tulip?" Roxanne asked.

Amanda sighed. "I don't have a clue."

She didn't even know why the Regal Beagle had come through the mirror. The little chubby dog was probably just looking for an all-you-can-eat buffet and didn't even realize she had gone back in time.

"Maybe they caught her," Roxanne said. "And...then..." She fell silent.

At the thought of the old dog being captured by the judge, shivers raced through the girls, just as they approached the house again. In deathly silence, the four of them crept into the neighboring yard and along the hedge that bordered the west edge of their house. Through a ragged gap torn through the foliage by the recent shotgun blast that had been meant for them, the girls spied Judge Blackburn. He was seated erect in a wicker chair on the front porch, a cigar lodged in the corner of his mouth and the shotgun resting diagonally in his lap.

The girls froze.

To their surprise, the judge was again talking with Constable Calhoun, who was standing on the wooden steps. "I got your message, Judge," the man said, "and headed straight back here."

"I need to have a word with you, Amos," Judge Blackburn said. "In private—about those gypsies."

"You know, Clement," the constable went on. "More than likely they're immigrants, right off the boat. I didn't get a good look at them, and with their funny clothes, it's hard to sort out all those strange folks. They sure ain't like us. But with so many of their kind around town these days, they got to be foreigners."

"I know," the judge said. "But as far as we're concerned, they're gypsies—and they stole two hundred dollars worth of gold coins and jewelry."

Constable Calhoun scowled. "Don't worry, sir, we'll hunt them down and lock them up in the calaboose for a good long time."

"I do not want them arrested," Judge Blackburn said in a low, ominous voice. "I want to be rid of them altogether."

"Rid of them?"

"And that lowdown boy who's in love with my Katie," Judge Blackburn went on. "If he were to get swept up in your hunt and 'dealt' with…you catch my drift."

"Judge, I can't just gun them down," the constable said. "Not in cold blood. That's murder. Even if they are lowlifes."

"But what if they're resisting arrest? Or they attack you? You have every right to use deadly force to enforce the law and protect yourself, Amos."

The constable mumbled, "I don't know, Judge. You described the females as little more than girls. Even the Polish boy, well, he can't be more than eighteen."

Gazing into the night sky, Judge Blackburn blew out a stream of cigar smoke. "I'm a respectable, upstanding man in Maysville. If folks knew that my daughter was cavorting with one of *them*, I'd become a laughingstock. Which is intolerable to me, especially as I am running for mayor. The scandal might very well cost me the election."

"No, you're sure to win, Judge," the constable insisted.

"Amos, it may come as a surprise to you, but over the years I've made quite a few enemies in our fair city. They'll say that if I can't manage my own family, how can I ever govern Maysville? But I'm determined to win this election, and as mayor, I want a constable upon whom I can depend."

Amos Calhoun shuffled his feet. "I've been the constable for fifteen years, sir."

"It would be a shame if you lost your job."

"Is that a threat?"

"Let me put it another way," Judge Blackburn said with a casual wave of his hand. "If you take care of this little problem for me, it's guaranteed that you'll keep your job for as long as I run this city. And you might even get a nice raise in recognition of your fine work."

"But why kill them?"

Judge Blackburn rolled the cigar in his mouth and peered back, his eyes narrowing to slits, as though sizing up the constable. "The girls," he hesitated, then continued, "may have witnessed a small indiscretion on my part." He coughed uneasily. "I was teaching the boy a lesson—with my buggy whip."

The constable chuckled. "Heck-fire, hardly a day goes by without me beating on one of them or some colored fella. No harm in thrashing one of *them*. Just between you and me, it's kind of fun."

"Just the same," Judge Blackburn explained. "I'm a pillar of the community. No point in sullying my reputation."

The real story, Amanda thought, was that the judge doesn't want anyone to report how he had ended up cowering before young Jan Brandowski, who had stood up to him.

"Didn't you tell me they had a little dog with them?"

The judge grumbled, "Mabel lit after that mutt with the hand ax, shrieking like a banshee. You know how she hates dogs and cats. As do I. She was about to send it to kingdom come when the boy raised a ruckus. Said he wanted to keep the dog as a pet. Can you imagine that?"

The judge sounded aghast at the idea of a pet. "Mabel won't deny the boy anything, so she obliged. But as soon as she turned her back, the dog vanished. The mutt is so fat that you can hardly imagine it could move so quickly, but it was nowhere to be found."

The judge bent forward in his rocking chair. "If you come across the dog, Amos, do me a small favor. Just shoot it."

"We already got too many strays in this town," Constable Calhoun agreed. "Not counting all the mongrels of the two-legged variety."

"The boy put out a bowl of table scraps, and that mutt may get hungry and come back. If it does, I myself will then blast it with my shotgun," Judge Blackburn went on. "Nothing I hate worse than a dog. Except a cat."

As the girls eavesdropped, Amanda dreaded that Tulip would catch a whiff of those leftovers and waddle back to beg for a handout.

Sally seethed. "That monster. He's an evil man."

"Shush," Roxanne warned.

"But he's gonna kill our dog," Sally whispered.

"And Judge Blackburn said we stole gold coins and jewelry from him," Josie whispered to the other girls clustered around her. "That's a lie!"

"Forget him—and Tulip for now," Amanda suggested. "Let's try around back while we have a chance."

She took a single step and immediately broke a twig underfoot.

Crack.

All four girls froze. Glancing toward the porch, they held their breath.

However, the judge and constable were so engrossed in their conversation that they hadn't heard the sound. The judge was saying something about the immigrant boy "knowing too much."

Amanda released a long sigh. "Whew."

Ever so cautiously, she and her sister and friends crept along the hedge to the back yard. The shrubs and flowerbeds were arranged differently, and there were so many outbuildings: garden shed, smokehouse, rootcellar, chicken coop, and outhouse. But at least Amanda was acquainted with the general layout of her own backyard.

She eased open the gate of a white picket fence by the corner of the house and winced as the hinges squeaked. But no one came to investigate the noise, so the four of them picked their way into the bushes clustered around the back porch.

No one was guarding the door, so they crept toward the back porch just as Judge Blackburn called from deep within the house, "Mabel, where are you?"

"Here in the kitchen," the woman answered.

She was no more than ten feet away.

Instinctively, the girls retreated into the bushes.

"That was close," Amanda whispered.

"She must be keeping an eye on the back door," Josie said.

"The constable tells me his men are on the way," Judge Blackburn told his wife. "Won't be long and he'll hunt those vagrants down and stick a gun in their faces."

Mabel Blackburn answered, "But they didn't steal anything, Clement. Why did you lie to Calhoun?"

"For the insurance money, Mabel," cackled the man, who by the sound of his voice was now drifting into the kitchen. "We'll file a claim and be two hundred dollars richer."

"You are so clever," the woman cooed. "They probably weren't even thieves—maybe just hungry and looking for some food, but—"

"Then why were they up in the attic? All immigrants have sticky fingers! It's part of their nature," the man thundered. "And they're probably Communists, too. I tell you, Mabel, they're the ruination of our country!"

"I thought we needed their labor. You sure worked that young man hard. He was a good stable hand, and so industrious and clever. He could fix anything."

"He scarcely spoke English!" the judge snapped. "And he comes to think he's good enough for a young lady like our precious Katie!"

"That is an outrage," Mabel Blackburn clucked. "I don't know what's come over the girl—falling in love with one of *them.*"

"We'll have to guard the house all night," the judge said. "In case that boy sneaks back here. I suspect that he and Katie want to elope. Those girls must be in cahoots with him, and probably plan to rob us while they're at it."

"I think those girls were up in the attic fetching some clothes for Katie. But we can't watch her night and day. Tomorrow I must go shopping, to the dry goods store and then over to the mercantile. I was hoping you'd drive me in the auto."

"I'll have someone take you in the buggy," the judge said.

"The boy also wants to stop by the nickelodeon. He's just fascinated by those new moving pictures."

"You may do as you please," Judge Blackburn said. "Come morning, we'll be rid of the boy and his accomplices."

Mabel Blackburn sighed, "I do hope that the constable will deport him and those girls back to their old country. If there are two words those people understand and fear it's 'deport' and 'constable.' I don't know much about that strange land he came from—they all speak such gibberish—but he most assuredly does *not* want to go back there. You could see the anguish in his eyes. But I still wonder if that will be enough to stop him."

The judge chuckled. "I'm afraid that my whip had little effect on him, even when I broke it over his back. But I've got my shotgun, which can surely help in *persuading* him and those tramps. I will guard the house until this mess is over."

"Can't the constable have a man do that for us?" Mabel asked.

Judge Blackburn replied, "He is guarding the front door for the moment, until his posse arrives and then he'll be off. But I don't want anyone else involved. Do you want word to get around that our daughter has taken up with one of *them?* Oh, the shame of it, Mabel!"

The woman clucked again. "You would think the girl would have more sense—and more respect for her parents."

"Don't worry, Mabel," Judge Blackburn said. "The constable and his rowdies will take care of everything. They'll assemble here. He'll give them their marching order and send them on their way—to roust that Jan Brandowski from his lodgings and send him to his Maker. And then he'll hunt down those girls and shoot them on sight. That'll fix the problem quite nicely, don't you think? Now it's late. Why don't you get some rest, my darling?"

"I am all aflutter. Perhaps I shall go to bed."

A chair scraped back as the portly woman apparently rose with a swish of long petticoats and skirt, and retired up the stairs.

Suddenly Judge Clement Blackburn strode out onto the back porch. The screen-door flapped shut behind him, and he stood there, shotgun in hand—right next to the bushes in which the girls were hidden.

Sally gasped.

The man glanced their way, startled.

The girls held their breath.

"Who's there?" the man growled, bringing the shotgun to his shoulder and aiming it right into the bushes. "Come out now—with your hands up!"

The girls froze.

"I'll blast you to smithereens!"

It's all over, Amanda thought.

She was about to step from the bushes, if only to save her sister and friends, when, just a few feet from them, Tulip ambled out of the thick bushes.

"Egad!" Judge Blackburn cried, jumping back.

"What is it, Clem?" Mabel called from the upstairs window.

The man chortled maliciously. "That sorry mongrel—of the four-legged variety."

"It must be hungry."

"Well, it gave me quite a fright."

"Shoot it!" Mabel Blackburn whispered down. "We don't

need another mangy dog pawing through the trash cans in the alley."

Without a word, Judge Blackburn pointed the shotgun at the plump beagle.

Amanda was about to rush at the judge when he paused and lowered the gun. "But, Mabel," he whispered. "I thought you told the boy he could keep the dog?"

"He's gone to bed," Mabel answered. "He won't be the wiser."

Judge Blackburn cocked the trigger.

Amanda was about to pounce and do whatever it took to save her dear fat little dog, but then she witnessed an unbelievable sight.

Not once in her life had Tulip ever moved faster than a slow-motion lope. But now the tri-colored sausage of a dog rocketed across the yard, sped around the corner of the smokehouse, and vanished into the night.

"Dang it," Judge Blackburn muttered.

A moment later, there was a commotion at the front of the house.

"The men are here!" Mabel called down. "Looks like Amos deputized half the men in town. Most are on horseback, but there are some buggies and a couple of Model T Fords sputtering down the street."

"It's about time." Judge Blackburn hustled back through the house to greet them.

"He almost shot my dog," Sally sputtered. "If she hadn't run away...."

Amanda whispered soothingly. "Tulip will be all right. She'll come back...."

But to herself she thought, *At least I hope she'll find her way back to us.*

"She saved us!" Josie muttered. "Tulip is brave and smart. She does have a sixth sense. I told you so."

"Let's just find that girl, Katie," Roxanne urged. "Find out what we need to do, jump back through that mirror, and get the heck out of here!"

"Just watch out for old lard lady—what's her name? Mabel Blackburn?" Josie cautioned.

As the girls crept up the back-porch steps, they peeked into the kitchen. No one was there. The woman had either gone to bed or joined her husband.

They could hear Judge Blackburn out on the front porch, lecturing the posse. "They are dangerous fugitives. So you are advised—correction—you are ordered to shoot first, and ask questions later."

While the man was occupied, the girls eased the screen-door open and slipped into the kitchen.

They were alone…thankfully.

Again awed and a little shocked by the charming decor of the house that contrasted with the vicious behavior of its occupants, the girls tiptoed through the kitchen. They crept past the pantry lined with jars of preserves, and the icebox.

Josie couldn't resist opening the door to peek at the large block of ice dripping into a pan and cooling the inside.

"Josie!" Roxanne gasped.

"Sorry," Josie muttered. "Just curious."

The girls crept to the doorway that led into the dining room with its dark, elegant furniture strewn with lace doilies.

Out on the porch, Judge Blackburn was still busy with the

posse, talking about keeping Maysville safe for women and children.

"We'll have to keep low. Crawl across the dining room and then go up the stairs," Amanda whispered. "Quietly."

On hands and knees, the girls scurried across the room to the staircase, with just a glance over their shoulders to the front porch.

So far, so good, Amanda thought. Ever so slowly, the girls made their way up the stairs, which creaked agonizingly with each step.

"What's that?" Mabel Blackburn muttered from the bedroom.

The girls froze once again.

"Clement, it that you?" the woman asked.

The lady of the house had indeed gone to bed, but the ruckus out front must have kept her awake.

Exposed in the open hallway, the girls stood like statues.

Downstairs, the judge had sent the posse on its way, and they could hear him stomping back into the house. Any moment, he might come up the stairs.

Or Mabel Blackburn would stumble out of her bedroom and scream bloody murder.

VI.

For several long minutes, the girls waited, frozen in the open hallway.

They could hear Judge Blackburn downstairs, apparently pacing from the parlor through the dining room and into the kitchen, back and forth, keeping a restless watch. Every time he returned to the parlor, the girls expected him to veer up the stairs to check on his wife and son. Meanwhile, they could hear Mrs. Blackburn tossing and turning on her overburdened bed. Every time she grunted, they likewise expected her to appear in the doorway, axe in hand, shouting for her husband.

And what about that bratty kid, Amanda wondered. When they'd encountered Orville Blackburn earlier that night, he'd had a smirk on his face and an evil glint in his beady eyes. He had probably gone to bed, but all the ruckus about the posse might have roused the little sneak who could be lurking anywhere in the shadows, ready to spring out and shriek, "Thieving gypsies!"

None of the girls had ever been this still for so long, thought Amanda, especially Sally, who was more accustomed to crashing around the house. Eventually, they could hear Mabel Blackburn drifting into sleep, gurgling through her nose. Soon she began to emit loud, choppy, wet snores.

Josie chuckled, "She sounds like a pig at a trough."

"Shush," Roxanne chastised. "That's no way to talk about an old lady."

But Amanda had to agree with Josie. Mabel Blackburn sounded like she was slurping down slops.

Tiptoeing past the old lady's bedroom, the girls hurried down the hall and peeked into Katie's room. As when they had seen her last—it seemed a long time ago—the young woman was sitting at her vanity, her face lit by a single candle, as if keeping a vigil.

Quietly stepping into the doorway, Amanda asked, "May we come in?"

Startled, her eyes blurred with tears, the girl glanced up and nodded.

The four visitors slipped into the room and eased the door closed behind them.

"Who are you?" Katie asked, wide-eyed, though unafraid. "Where did you come from?"

Amanda said, "That's a long story. And you would never believe us."

"Aren't you friends of Jan?"

"In a way," Amanda said. "We want to help you."

Katie glanced aside. She seemed to be studying the swirl pattern of her bedspread. Then she spoke, with a sigh of despair. "No one can help me. I am in love with Jan, but now it is over. Father has driven him away. He is going back to Chicago to live with his brother. This very night he will leave on the train."

"Why did your father drive him away?" Josie asked, although the girls already knew the answer.

Katie sighed. "We wish to be married. But Jan is a foreigner, and I am an American. What country are you from?"

"We're Americans, too," Amanda answered.

Katie managed a wisp of a smile. "But you dress as though you come from a strange and faraway land."

"All of our ancestors were immigrants," Josie explained. "And yours were too."

"My father tells me we are of English descent," Katie said. "Which is the best kind of ancestry, he says. Father insists that I marry one of our own kind, as he puts it."

Having heard enough about the judge, Amanda urged, "Tell us about Jan."

"He moved here from Chicago last year," Katie explained. "Jan wanted a job in the zinc foundry, or the brickyards, but they weren't hiring. So father employed him to take care of the horses and to do odd jobs. He is such an industrious and clever worker that he became our gardener, carpenter, and handyman, as well as being so good with the animals.

"He was very grateful. He said in his country he would have to work all day for a few pennies or a loaf of bread—if he could find any work at all. But in America he could earn enough to eat and send money to his family in Poland so they wouldn't starve. He has two brothers in Chicago, but another brother and sisters and cousins in Poland who want to come here, too. He was saving money to buy tickets for them so they could take a ship to Ellis Island, just as his two older brothers did for him.

"Jan is so strong and handsome and caring—how could I *not* fall in love with him? He is quickly learning English and has great ambitions. In the old country, his family had a small estate, where they raised fine horses.

"But there was much danger from those Russian revolution-aries and Cossacks, who often raided their farm, taking whatever they wanted. Jan and his family had to hide out in a cave in the forest. It became so dangerous that they had to abandon their estate and flee for their lives. They lost everything.

"What does it matter if Jan is not an American? He yearns to become a proud citizen and he is a *human being*. And we love each other so much." Her voice trembled, and she paused.

"For the longest time Mama and Papa didn't suspect us," Katie continued. "Then Jan gave me the most beautiful mirror."

Amanda's eyebrows went up. "Mirror?"

"Yes. It is finely crafted; oval-shaped, with crinkled edges. But, alas, when Papa found out, he seized it. He shattered the mirror to pieces, he told me, to teach me a lesson, because I was so vain. But I know he was just angry because the mirror was a gift from Jan."

"Uh, I don't think he broke your mirror," Amanda said.

"How so?" Katie asked.

"I think we've sort of seen it—in the attic."

Josie snorted, "We've more than *seen* it."

"Pardon me?" Katie asked.

Amanda shot a glance at her friend.

Josie shrugged. "Just say we've been *through* a lot tonight."

Katie looked puzzled. She frowned and went on, "I should have known Papa would not destroy the mirror. He has such a lust for money. He must have hid it in the attic until he has time to sell it, without my knowledge, only to pocket the money for himself."

"You can marry Jan if you want," Josie said. "It's your life. You can do whatever you want."

"Not without my parents' blessing," Katie gasped. "And Papa has forbidden me to see Jan. I cannot disobey him or Mama."

"Hey, Josie is right. It's 1912!" Amanda pointed out, although still mystified that they had actually gone so far back in time. "It's a new century—a new era. You're free to choose your own husband."

"That's unthinkable!"

"Believe me, honey," Josie went on. "Before long, you'll be voting in elections and all kinds of stuff."

Katie stared at them, wide-eyed. "You sound like Teddy Roosevelt and his Republicans, and now that Bull Moose Party. They say women should have the right to vote. They even put it in their platform. Father says it is unladylike for women to trouble themselves with politics and working outside the home, unless they are servants or factory girls."

Overcoming her fear, Roxanne spoke up. "You'll see, soon women will have all kinds of jobs."

"We may teach school, but only if we are not married, of course," Katie mused. "And a woman can become a librarian. But the widows and others must take in laundry, or serve as maids or cooks. Of course, some find work as factory girls. It is a low and mean life."

"Factory girls?" Josie asked.

"Just last year," Katie said mournfully, "more than a hundred and forty-six of five hundred girls who worked in the Triangle Shirtwaist Factory burned to death in a fire in New York City. Surely you read about it in the newspaper. They couldn't escape the flames, because they were locked in the factory during their workshift. How ghastly. Who would want such a life?"

"I read about that, too, but not exactly last year," Amanda

said. "My dad talked to me about the tragedy. He said it has become a symbol of terrible sweatshop working conditions."

Katie sighed, "Father says it didn't matter much, because the girls were only immigrants. He says those poor girls had less value than slaves, because when they died, the factory owners lost nothing. They simply hired other starving immigrants who desperately needed work."

"Trust me, life in America will get better," Amanda said. "I am sure that one day, women will enter every profession—as doctors, scientists, and business leaders."

"And you can play sports!" Sally burst.

"Of all the foolishness!" Katie gasped. "Why would I want to participate in athletic competitions? It is unladylike."

Amanda couldn't help saying, "The way Sally plays sure is 'unladylike'."

"Hey!" Sally said. "I can kick any boy's butt, that's true."

"Shame on you," Katie said. "Girls do *not* play sports, except for pleasant yard games like croquet and badminton. Besides, boys are so much stronger than we—and more sensible, too."

Josie quipped, "I'd like to find just one boy who had a lick of sense."

"You'll see," Roxanne told Katie. "You have a lot to look forward to in your lifetime."

Amanda counseled, "And you should marry Jan, if you want to."

"But he is leaving on the night train, and he's never coming back to this town."

"Then go after him," Josie urged.

Katie was horrified. "But I'm a lady! I cannot approach a man. I must wait for him to come courting."

"That's ridiculous," Josie said. "You can go right up to any dumb guy and talk to him."

"Really?"

Roxanne hitched her thumb toward Josie. "Believe me, Josie knows what she's talking about. She's, like, boy crazy."

"I did visit alone with Jan," Katie admitted, "when we should have been properly chaperoned."

"We'll find Jan for you," Amanda said. "And convince him to come back to you."

"But you're ladies, too."

"We're modern ladies," Amanda explained. "Is the train station where it's always been?"

"How silly," Katie said. "There's only one train station, and of course it's where it's always been. It's almost brand new. It was constructed in 1910."

Amanda thought of the old and grimy station, now served by Amtrak, and concluded that it had to be the same depot. "We'll have to hurry," she told her companions. "If Jan leaves, we'll have no way of ever finding him in Chicago."

"We'll run all the way!" Sally cried.

"Take the trolley!" Katie advised. "It is so fast—almost eight miles an hour, I've heard. So, hold on to your hats, ladies!"

Josie raised a hand. "Wait a sec. Katie *has* to come with us."

"She can't," Roxanne said.

"Yes, she *can,*" Amanda realized. "In fact, she has to."

"Why?" Katie asked.

Amanda looked around at the others, and then fixed her gaze on Katie. "It's too dangerous for Jan to come back here. Your father or one of his thugs will murder him. You will have to stand up for yourself, Katie. Now is the time to get away and elope, if that's what you want to do. If you truly love Jan, come with us and then leave with Jan on that train."

Amanda expected a refusal, or at least hesitation. But to everyone's astonishment, Katie sprang to her feet and proclaimed, "Indeed, I will. To hell with Father!"

The girls glanced at each other and smiled. *Where did that come from?* Amanda wondered. Katie must have been doing quite a lot of thinking, sitting for hours in her room, before they showed up.

"Atta girl," Josie said.

"Let's go," Roxanne warned. "Before someone overhears us."

"But I must pack."

"No time," Amanda said.

"Oh my, oh my." Katie seemed so excited that she had actually decided to act for herself.

Glancing each way down the hall, they eased out of the bedroom. While Mabel Blackburn snored away, the girls crept past her room and descended the stairs.

Although thrilled to serve as matchmaker for Katie and Jan, Amanda realized that she and her friends and sister were risking their lives. Judge Blackburn would shoot them on sight. If Constable Calhoun snatched them, they would not be jailed—they would be gunned down.

All was quiet downstairs. The front porch was vacant. Maybe Judge Blackburn had left to catch up with the posse and lead the manhunt—or *girl hunt.*

"Out the front door," Amanda whispered to the others. "Hurry!"

One after another, moving swiftly, they slipped outside.

"Whew," Roxanne exhaled as they hurried across the porch

and down the steps.

Josie grinned. "Piece of cake."

No sooner were the words out of her mouth than a black shadow sprang in front of them and let out a blood-curdling scream.

All five girls recoiled.

"Here they are, Papa!" Orville Blackburn squealed. "Dirty gypsies!"

Wielding a baseball bat and bouncing with malign delight, he confronted the pack of girls on the front sidewalk. "I've found them! Papa, come quick!"

Everyone froze, except Sally.

To Amanda's surprise, the scrappy girl rushed right up to the brat and let loose with a haymaker punch that connected with the boy's nose. The baseball bat flew out of Orville's hands and rattled on the pavement as he landed hard on his behind.

"Papa, Mama!" Orville shrieked. "Help! Murder!"

Scrambling backwards across the lawn to get away from Sally, he demanded, "What kind of ladies are you?"

"The kind that beats the snot out of crybabies like you," Josie retorted.

Fists clenched, Sally said, "And if you don't shut up, I'll knock the teeth right out of your head."

For a moment, the boy cringed, then he squealed with malicious joy and pointed behind the girls.

To their shock and horror, none other than the constable and several men were rushing from hiding places in the bushes along each side of the house. Brandishing rifles, shotguns, and clubs, the men surged toward the front yard. "Shoot them!" Judge Blackburn yelled as he lumbered around the corner.

The girls raced away as wild gunfire rang out into the night—the blasts of shotguns, the sharp cracks of single-shot rifles, and the ping of pistols. The bullets and shotgun pellets whizzed through the air, tearing through the branches of the trees in the yard, and shredding the leaves or thudding into tree trunks.

Orville caterwauled, "Father, they're kidnapping Katie!"

"Hold fire, you fools! Hold fire!" Judge Blackburn roared.

The shooting ceased, as the men realized Katie was fleeing with the other girls.

Everyone just stood there and gaped after them.

"This way!" Amanda exclaimed.

Before the men awoke from their stupor, the girls rushed down the street.

Amanda glanced over her shoulder. Lowering their weapons, the men looked at the judge in confusion.

"Sorry, Judge," someone mumbled. "You told us to shoot them."

"Didn't you blockheads see Katie was with them?" Clement Blackburn thundered. "You idiots could have killed her."

There was an eerie moment of calm before the judge erupted, "Don't just stand there, you numbskulls! They've made off with my daughter. Catch them!"

Behind them Amanda heard the sounds of running feet, then the sputter of Model Ts and the clatter of hooves on the brick street as the men clambered into automobiles and mounted their horses, and charged after them.

At least Amanda knew the neighborhood well—or hoped she did. But she didn't see how they could get to the train station without being caught, not with this mob hot on their heels.

The girls sprinted down Elm and cut right at Orchard Street

in the neighborhood of what was now Old Town in Maysville, except that everything here was new. The clapboard on the houses that flashed past gleamed with new paint.

"We can't outrun them!" Roxanne exclaimed.

"Gotta get off the sidewalk," Josie urged.

"This way!" Amanda cried out and the girls veered down the alley that ran behind the row of houses on Elm Street.

"Ow!" Sally exclaimed as the girls ran barefoot over the cinders and ashes from coal stoves and furnaces.

"Run along the side," Amanda said. "It's mostly weeds."

"We've got to hide," Josie insisted. "Over here."

The girls squatted next to a garden shed and some trash barrels, just as the mob swept down Orchard Street and slowed to a confused stop.

"Where'd they go?" someone asked.

"They vanished," another guy said. "Into thin air."

"They're gypsies. They know black magic!"

"Don't be a fool."

"Here's a footprint!"

Amanda crossed her fingers and prayed, *Please, please, don't let them turn down the alley.*

"Down the alley!" another man piped.

"We've got to hide better!" Amanda whispered. "Here!"

She and the other girls wedged themselves into a slender gap between the garden shed and a board fence, as the clot of men clamored down the alley.

For a long moment, the girls held their breath. Amanda squeezed her eyes shut, hoping that might somehow make her less visible.

The small mob rumbled past them. The girls waited until

their hooting and hollering dwindled in the distance.

"That was close," Roxanne whispered as they snuck out from behind the shed.

"My goodness, what a frightening adventure!" Katie exclaimed. "Are you young ladies in the habit of fleeing for your lives?"

"Only when we have to," Josie said.

Amanda glanced around the alley at all the wooden sheds and backyard gardens. The neighborhood wasn't much different from the present, she thought, except that every backyard seemed to have a large vegetable garden, complete with a manure pile. And most yards had a chicken coop tucked in a back corner, along with an outhouse.

It might appear that little had changed, but Amanda knew from her grandma's stories that ice wagons once rolled down these alleys. Her grandma and the other kids had raced after the wagons in hopes that the iceman would throw chips of ice to them as he gripped each block with a pair of tongs, swung it over his shoulder, lugged it into the kitchen of each house, and deposited it in the icebox.

"We were always up to something," Grandma recalled warmly. "Just like the Little Rascals."

Amanda had always thought of those times as the "good old days." Her grandparents had been sweet, kindly people. She suspected that most people back then were good-hearted, not like Judge Blackburn and that angry mob. They had just stumbled through the mirror into a hornets' nest of hatred and intolerance.

Sally whispered, "I'm scared."

"I know," Amanda said. "But I'll look after you."

Josie chuckled, "After seeing how Sally decked that Orville kid, I'd say she can take care of herself."

Roxanne appeared to be too frightened to utter a word.

But Josie was unfazed. "Those guys will never catch us. They're idiots!"

The girls had dodged their pursuers for the moment, but Katie warned, "Those men are dangerous."

They're also armed to the teeth and itching to shoot at us, Amanda thought. Now the alarm was not only for "thieving gypsies," but also "kidnappers."

Her little sister had lapsed back into wide-eyed terror, but Amanda assured her, "We can make it, Sally—as long as we're careful."

Josie snorted, "Luckily, those guys make such a racket we can hear them a mile away."

"They're not too smart either," Roxanne managed to say.

"Let's go," Amanda said. "But keep an eye out."

The girls continued west down the alley, a cinder occasionally digging into their bare feet. At the end of the block, they turned down Hickory Avenue and zigzagged down some side streets.

"Wait," Katie exclaimed.

Amanda thought that the young woman needed a rest. Katie had been racing along with them, stride for stride, although she had bunched her long skirts in her hands and had to stumble along on clunky, high-topped shoes. Or maybe she had changed her mind about going after Jan.

Katie said, "We'll never get to the train station in time."

Everyone wilted.

"But we have to try," Josie insisted.

Katie shook her head. "That's not what I mean. We can't

run all the way. We'll have to take the trolley, and hurry. It's our only chance."

Amanda figured that the trolley ran down Main Street, because even in her day the tracks remained on the brick pavement as a memento of the past. But she wasn't sure.

Then it occurred to her that Katie already knew the way. "Okay," Amanda said. "Katie, we'll follow you."

The girls traveled as fast as they could for about five blocks, heading north, but hesitated as they came to Main Street. It was late, but the area was illuminated with streetlamps, and there were a lot of people milling around downtown. Anyone there might have heard about the girls who were wanted as "thieving gypsies" and "kidnappers."

Do we dare step out into the bright lights of this street, Amanda wondered.

"Quickly," Katie exclaimed. "Jan's train leaves at midnight."

A trolley was just turning the corner off Broadway.

It's now or never, Amanda thought.

The trolley slowed to a stop at the corner of Main and Goodwin streets.

"Wait!" Katie shouted to the conductor and rushed across the street.

Drawing long breaths and hoping that no one would identify them, the girls sprinted after Katie and jumped aboard the clanging car just as it sped up.

"Five cents," the conductor scowled at them beneath the bill of his cap as they mounted the steps.

"Oh no!" Amanda groaned.

She dug into the pocket of the shorts that she wore under her dress and to her relief found that she had a nickel, which she handed to the conductor.

As she was rummaging in her pocket for more change to pay for Sally and her friends, the conductor studied the coin and then squinted at Amanda. "Hey, what's the big idea?"

Amanda gasped as she realized that the design of coins had changed, and the date was more than a hundred years in the future!

"What do you mean?" Amanda asked, wondering if they would have to jump off the trolley and run for their lives again.

With a puzzled look on his whiskered face, the conductor demanded, "You trying to pull a fast one? We don't take no foreign coinage on this trolley, missy."

Amanda sighed with relief.

"Sorry!" she cried, snatching the coin back from his open palm.

Reaching out his hand, the conductor said, "Lemme have another look at it, will ya?"

"That's okay," Amanda said, tucking the nickel back into her pocket.

Glaring at her, the conductor hit the brakes on the trolley, which screeched to a stop. "No fare, then get off my trolley!" he grumbled. "We don't tolerate no freeloaders."

"Here!" Katie said, rushing forward and handing some coins to the conductor that she'd dug out of a small change purse. Amanda only had a glance, but they appeared to be three Liberty Head nickels and a Barber dime.

"Friends of yours, are they, Miss Blackburn?" the conductor asked, a hint of scorn in his voice.

"Yes." Katie's chin rose a notch. "Yes, they are."

"Humph," the conductor snorted. "To each his own."

But he turned the lever without further delay, and the trolley rattled down the tracks, sparks occasionally flaring from the electrical wire overhead.

As the girls walked down the aisle and sat down on wooden seats, Katie whispered, "Luckily, I had my change purse. I'd almost forgotten it was in my pocket. I'm in such a tizzy. I'm afraid I'm not at all prepared for this…this journey into the unknown."

Try going back in time a hundred years, Amanda thought, but she only smiled back at Katie. "You'll do fine."

Josie fumed. "That conductor is a creep."

"Everybody thinks we're foreigners because we're dressed like this," Roxanne said.

"I'd like punch that guy in the stomach," Sally said.

Josie laughed. "You sure have a scrappy little sister, Amanda."

"She's hell on wheels," Amanda agreed. "Except when she's scared of everything."

In the distance, they heard the sounds of bells. It must be the courthouse, Amanda thought. She counted the rings…ten, eleven, twelve. "It's midnight!" she cried.

Could the night have flown by so quickly?

Katie drew her small lady's watch from a pocket and gasped, "The train leaves in minutes and Jan will be on board! I'll never see him again. I don't know where his brother lives in Chicago. I'll never be able to find him again if we don't catch him before he leaves!"

"Can't this thing speed up?" Sally scowled. "I could have been to the train station and back on my mountain bike by now."

"But this is still pretty cool," Josie said, gazing around at the passing shops on either side of them. "Everything is so old-timey."

"No, it isn't!" Roxanne gasped. "It's a nightmare."

Given the late hour, there were only a handful of people riding the trolley, but with her outburst, the men glared at the girls and the women peeked from behind fluttering fans. Luckily, it appeared that none of them had heard the news that the constable and his deputies were hunting for a group of girls.

As the trolley rumbled along the Main Street, Amanda glimpsed many familiar buildings still part of modern Maysville, except that these brick and stone facades appeared relatively new. And several unfamiliar enterprises lined the street—a drugstore and fountain, café, livery stable (where an auto garage now stood), bank, law offices, dry goods store, and a mercantile. There was also an opera house and a nickelodeon where the Rialto movie theater now stood.

It was strange, watching the buildings go by as they clattered along on the trolley. It reminded her of a small diorama of a turn-of-the-century American town that she had once viewed at the state museum.

Although fascinated by the old cityscape, Amanda and the other girls desperately wanted to get to the train station on the west side of Maysville—for Katie's sake and their own. But the trolley rolled along at an agonizingly slow pace, stopping at one corner and then another.

At long last, the trolley dipped through the underpass that went under the railroad tracks, just to the south of the station.

"There's the station," Sally announced.

"How do you stop this thing?" Josie asked.

In answer, Katie reached up and pulled one of the ropes that ran along each side, just above the row of windows, and rang a jangling bell.

The trolley ground to a halt. Without missing a beat, the girls rushed out the door at the intersection of Main and Chester streets.

A variety of shops that catered to travelers and folks who lived in the neighborhood, then informally known as West Maysville, lined Chester Street. Across from the station, Amanda noticed a hotel, café, ice cream parlor, tobacconist, clothier, and small opera house for vaudeville shows. There was a livery stable down a side street, and several warehouses along both sides of the railroad tracks.

There were quite a few people clustered on Chester Street— probably awaiting the arrival of the train. Several folks paused to gawk at the girls.

"What's the world coming to?" asked an old man, centering himself on his cane. "Girls running around barefoot in gaudy clothes. I never!"

"Go on home!" an elderly woman hissed at them.

"Back to your own neighborhood in the Bottoms," her companion added.

A man with a handlebar moustache stepped out of the tobacconist shop, paused next to a wooden cigar store Indian, and lit a thick stogie. As he shook out his match and took a long puff, he studied the girls. "Hey, aren't those the gypsies the constable is looking for? Stop them!"

Everyone on the street became alarmed, as though a bomb had been thrown into their midst.

"Help! Call the police!" a skinny man in straw hat and tweed suit shouted, as he raced around the corner.

Everyone in the crowd stared intently at the girls as they eased toward the station. A few tried to block their way, but the girls nimbly scooted around them. Amanda hoped that the constable and his posse were not nearby.

But moments later, a policeman in dark blue uniform, Bismarck helmet, and knee-high leather boots trotted around the corner on a tall, bay horse.

Running beside him was the man in the straw hat. "Over there, Deputy Harrigan!" he cried, pointing at the five girls.

Yanking a Billy club from his belt, the deputy spurred his horse and shouted, "Stop, in the name of the law!"

The girls did the opposite. Turning on their heels, they fled down Chester Street and cut around the railroad station.

Swinging the nightstick in his right hand, the deputy hunkered down in the saddle and raced after them.

VII.

As the girls sprinted around the train station and toward the tracks, Katie screamed, "Watch out! The train is pulling into the station!"

The girls skidded to a stop.

Indeed, smoke billowing from its stacks, a huge steam engine was bearing down on them.

Behind them Amanda heard the clatter of hooves on the brick pavement. There was no way that the girls could outrun a horse. Moments later, the deputy was nearly upon them, and he now gripped a long-barreled pistol.

"Halt or I'll shoot!" he shouted.

Amanda sized up the train, especially its speed. "Hurry!" she urged. Without another word, the girls rushed into the white clouds of steam wafting around the wheels of the approaching engine and shot across the tracks—right in front of the train's cowcatcher.

Safely on the other side, the girls paused to get their breath.

"We dodged him," Josie said.

"For now," Katie observed. "But he'll be after us again as

soon as the train stops."

The girls scrambled onto another platform, which was cluttered with wooden boxes, crates, and leather-strapped trunks stacked on and near a row of wagons used for unloading freight.

But Amanda stopped short. She had lost sight of her little sister.

"Where's Sally?" Amanda gasped in horror.

She glanced into the steam pouring from the huge locomotive. She had assumed that her little sister, the soccer star, would sprint across the tracks faster than any of them, but maybe fear had frozen her in mid-stride. *Please God, not on the tracks,* Amanda prayed.

"She's right here!" Roxanne pointed behind the cluster of girls. With her hands over her face, stuck dumb with terror, Sally stood there, trembling.

"Thank God!" Amanda released the longest-held breath of her life. Once again she blamed herself for endangering her sister and friends in this strange place. She should have told them about the scary noises she had been hearing at night in her house. That should have been enough warning to avoid the mysterious mirror. Maysville might be their hometown, sleepy enough, it had always seemed to the girls, but in the past it had not been such an idyllic world.

"There's the cop!" Josie shouted.

Sure enough, the deputy had dismounted. Waving his pistol, he was looking here and there for the girls on the other side of the tracks. As the train came to a full stop, the man in uniform began to clamber over the coupler that connected two passenger cars.

"Quick!" Amanda exclaimed. "We've got to hide!"

The girls slipped into a little nook among the crates, barrels, and trunks stacked on the platform. They wedged themselves into a little corner and held their breaths.

The deputy looked up and down the railroad track. Then he headed in their direction. As he approached their hiding place, his footsteps slowed, then stopped.

The girls tensed.

"I know you're in there somewhere," he called out.

The girls were squeezing each others' hands tightly, each of them trying to will herself and the others to be brave.

This cannot be happening, Amanda thought. Then, to her horror, she felt a sneeze coming on. All the dust they had kicked up in scrambling into this little nook was tickling in her nose.

Unsure exactly where the girls might be hiding, the deputy turned away, just as Amanda let loose a powerful sneeze, "*Achoo!*"

The man spun around; the girls tensed.

It's all over, Amanda thought. But then the train whistled, and a man ran up, shouting, "They went that way, Charlie! Some folks saw 'em run into that big warehouse."

"Are you sure?" the deputy growled.

Through a gap in the wooden crates, Amanda glimpsed a man in a sack suit and bowler hat. The man replied, "Four girls in colorful clothes? Who else would it be, Charlie? The fools wouldn't be hanging around here, waiting for the train."

The deputy shouted, "Round up some able-bodied men and have them follow me—and make sure they're armed. I hear tell they're dangerous."

"Not my job," the man responded. "Besides, looked to me like those girls were frightened out of their wits. You ought to be ashamed of yourself, Charlie."

"I've got my orders," the deputy grunted.

"Doesn't mean you have to follow them."

Without another word, the deputy turned away from the man and strode toward a sprawling brick warehouse about a block down the railroad tracks.

The man tipped his bowler hat and winked in the direction of the girls. Then, whistling a tune, he ambled on his way.

"Why did that man do that?" Josie asked. "He was so nice."

Amanda shrugged. "Maybe there were a few good people back in the 'good old days'."

"There are many fine people in Maysville," Katie insisted. "Most are not like my...uh...parents." Then she suddenly cried out, "Jan!"

Amanda thought that perhaps Katie had spied her beloved, but then she realized, to her dismay, that the train was pulling away from the station.

"We're too late!" Katie wailed.

Amanda thought they might chase after the train, but it had already picked up too much speed. Plumes of white smoke poured from the nose of the engine as the train vanished into the night.

Creeping out from behind the boxes, the girls stood on the freight platform and gazed down the tracks.

Katie cried, "He's gone." She sank to her knees, weeping.

Amanda was shocked. They had come so close, only to miss the train.

She recalled one of her father's stories about her great-grandfather, who had left Slovenia and traveled across Europe with his fiancée. However, when the young couple arrived on the coast of France, they realized they had tickets for different ships. They sailed across the Atlantic Ocean separately. He had hoped they would meet when they arrived in New York, but he lost his bride-to-be in the throngs of thousands of people arriving at Ellis Island. He never found her again.

Amanda's great-grandfather, whom everyone called Old Joe, had been brokenhearted. But such were the twists of fate. If he had not lost his first love, he would never have married their great-grandmother, Amanda realized. She, Sally, and their baby brother Jacob would never have been born.

Katie rose to her feet, stood like a statue, and moaned, "All is lost!"

Amanda could not believe that for a moment. So much of love, so much of history itself could have been different, she reasoned. Yet nothing happened by chance. Somehow, millions of travelers came here, married, and had children, and confidently built their lives in the great waves of European migration to this land where the streets were said to be "paved with gold," but in truth were paved by hard work and sweat.

It had been destiny, she decided, that her family had moved into the old Victorian house that had stood empty for so long. It had been no accident that her mother had been drawn to the strange mirror, even as the old man had warned her of its danger. And the girls had been so curious about its magic.

Could that be the significance of the mirror—that the girls would be doomed if they tried to meddle with history, to mismatch a couple? What if Katie was *not* meant to be her friend John's great-grandmother? If Amanda interfered, wouldn't she be arranging for the boy never to be born?

No. It couldn't be wrong. Katie and her Polish suitor, Jan, were surely the answer to the mysterious question of which path of history was the right one.

The Jan of 1912 too closely resembled her classmate of a hundred years later. He *had* to be John Brandowski's great-grandfather. And she, Amanda Tucker, was meant to be their matchmaker. Somehow. Or else her John will never be born.

"That's why we're here," she muttered. "To help Katie and Jan run away and get married. So why have we failed?"

"Uh…guys," Josie said.

Everyone glanced at her.

The tall girl pointed north, up the tracks, in the direction from which the train had *come.* "Chicago is that way."

It took the girls a moment to realize the implication of what Josie was saying. "That's the train *from* Chicago," she exclaimed. "It's headed south to New Orleans!"

Everyone was ecstatic. Even Katie stopped weeping and looked up with a glimmer of hope.

"That's right," Amanda cried. "That train is even called the City of New Orleans, at least it is now. And the train *to* Chicago probably hasn't arrived yet."

"Maybe it's running late," Roxanne suggested.

Katie brightened. "Yes! The train used to be called the Chicago and New Orleans Limited. But just months ago, it was renamed the Panama Limited in honor of the great canal that will be completed next year! And yes, that train often does run late!"

Amanda thought about the Amtrak trains of the present day that usually lumbered into the station hours behind schedule. Some things never changed.

"Then Jan may still be in the station, waiting for his train," Katie exclaimed.

Rising to her feet, she grasped her skirt to raise the hem a little and started toward the train station. After a few steps, she paused. "Oh no, I'm a lady. I cannot waltz into that station alone. Not at night, without an escort."

"But you've come this far," Amanda pointed out.

"Come on," Josie urged. "We'll be your escort."

Roxanne objected, "But we can't be seen in public! By now everyone must know about the crazy gypsies."

Josie shrugged. "Maybe they assume we ran away and wouldn't dare try to walk into the train station in plain sight."

"I'm not so sure," Amanda said.

"Katie should go in by herself," Roxanne insisted.

"But we've come this far," Amanda said. "I'd like to see this through to the end."

Roxanne still wasn't convinced, and it took the girls a while to dislodge Sally, who was reluctant to leave her hidey-hole.

"No guts, no glory," Josie said. "Just imagine you're playing soccer, taking out some trash-talkin' kid on the other team."

They slipped across the train tracks to the passenger platform, not a soul in sight, until a shadow swept over them. It was the deputy on horseback. The girls ducked behind a baggage cart.

The deputy loped right past them, not even glancing their way, and continued south along the tracks. He was intent on inspecting the dark corners of the warehouses, including the spot in which they had just been hiding.

"Hurry!" Amanda urged. "Before anyone else comes by."

"Here goes nothing," Roxanne sighed, and the girls eased into the brightly-lit station.

Amanda was amazed.

The waiting room had the same décor as in the present day, minus the layers of dust and grime. The mint-green paint on the walls was bright and fresh. The marble columns sparkled, and the tall stylish benches glistened with new varnish. The same ornate bars graced the windows of the ticket counter, except that the new brass gleamed.

Thankfully, the waiting room was almost deserted, except for a few people waiting for the Chicago train and a couple of stragglers who had probably arrived on the last train. They were toting suitcases and bags out the doors to waiting horse carriages and Model Ts in what was now the taxi stand.

The girls scanned the long wooden benches, but Jan was nowhere in sight.

"He's not here," Katie whispered.

Maybe the constable caught him, Amanda thought, but she said nothing.

Sally spoke up, "How about the restaurant?"

At the far end of the station, a lively crowd had gathered in a café to enjoy a late dinner or cup of coffee and wedge of apple pie as they waited for the train.

"We cannot possibly go into that rough place," Katie said as the girls hurried across the floor in that direction. "It is not a proper place for a lady."

Through the open doorway and interior windows, the girls noted that only men congregated there. Remarkably, all the white men sat at wire-framed chairs and tables with glass tops, while the black men had to stand at the marble-topped counter. Amanda recalled her father once telling her that there had been discrimination not only in the South, but also in northern towns like Maysville. There may not have been actual Jim Crow laws, but there was a long, sad tradition of segregation. It meant that many shops and stores had signs reading "Whites Only" or "No Colored." Black people had to sit in the balcony at the movie theaters and they had not been allowed to even enter soda fountains.

Black people had to live in the Bottoms, which had originally been the immigrant community, so they went to their own grade school. Everyone went to the same high school, which wasn't segregated because it was the only one in town. But photos of black students were published separately, at the back of the yearbook. Amanda had been shocked when her father told her that it had been that way for decades—until the 1950s.

Among the customers at the station café, the girls noticed a young guy with blond hair, standing at the counter among the black men, in striking contrast to the rich brown skin of the other people who had to eat their pie and sip their coffee standing up.

Even if Katie had not gasped and whispered, "Jan," to the other girls, Amanda would have recognized the young man. She also noticed how he appeared to be the object of ridicule of the seated patrons, who pointed at him and guffawed beneath their handlebar moustaches.

"Can't tell himself from the colored," one man in gray pin-striped suit and derby sniggered.

"Dumb as an ox. Just like all the other immigrants," another guy agreed.

Clamping his teeth down on his cigar, a third man joked, "At least he knows his place."

However, Jan appeared to be oblivious to the ridicule as he leaned on the counter. Standing in the doorway, Amanda and the girls were uncertain what to do next.

"We can't possibly go in there," Katie emphasized.

"Why not?" Josie muttered. "This is so silly." It looked like she was ready to charge into the café, but Josie turned to Amanda instead and urged, "Go ahead."

"Me?" Amanda asked.

Josie shrugged. "Sure. You're more likely to behave yourself. I'm not sure what I would do if one of those idiots at the tables said the wrong thing."

No point in squabbling with Josie, Amanda thought. And her friend was right. All of them didn't need to go into the café and draw even more attention. Amanda sighed, then stood tall and walked into the café.

Conspicuous in her dress-up clothes, she hoped that these men had been there a while and had not heard about those "gypsy thieves." Still, as she strolled into the café, everyone fell silent, as if the sound had been sucked from the room. She felt all eyes upon her, as tangibly as if she were being jabbed by sharpened sticks.

"No ladies allowed in here!" a man grumbled.

"She's not a lady," another chided. "Just a dumb immigrant. Look at those foreign clothes. She don't know no better."

"Don't you know you're in the wrong place, girlie?" someone smirked. "Get out of here!"

Ignoring them, Amanda continued over to the counter, and leaned in next to Jan, trying to look relaxed, like she had just wandered in for a late-night bottle of soda pop. Out of the side of her mouth, she whispered to the Polish youth, "Jan, I have to talk with you!"

The young man stared at Amanda with a puzzled look. Again she noticed how deeply his blue eyes were set in his broad face, above his high cheekbones. Those eyes were slightly elliptical, just enough to lend a mystique to his appearance, as though he had come from distant lands, as he most truly had.

"Talk?" he asked in heavily accented English, his voice deep and resonant, as though the strength in his hands and shoulders flowed in rhythm with his words. "You speak the English?"

"Yes!" Amanda exclaimed. She nodded to the doorway. "We must leave this place. Now! Please!" She looked down at her own trembling hands.

Without another word, like an obliging child, Jan picked his cap off the counter, and followed her out of the café.

"Look at that!" someone called after them. "His baby sister found him lost again and has come to fetch him home."

"Good riddance to bad rubbish," someone cackled after them.

Ignoring them, Amanda hustled out of the café with Jan, whose eyes were full of wonder, though he walked with a confident step.

Outside, Amanda quickened her step. "Whew."

"I do not know you," Jan said. "What do you want of me?"

"I'll show you."

Amanda glanced around the waiting room. Her sister, friends, and Katie had vanished. Where could they have gone? Had the deputy snatched them?

Trying to control her panic, Amanda mumbled, "Katie sent me."

"Katie?"

"Yes!" Amanda answered with growing anxiety. "She was right here…a moment ago."

Although she did not know Jan Brandowski—this young man from another time—Amanda sensed that she could trust him. Perhaps it was his eyes, so intelligent, yet innocent. Or the manner in which he carried himself, so politely and so full of grace.

The young man stood erect and declared, "I do not know what..." He paused, then said, "I am going home."

"To Chicago?" Amanda asked.

Jan shook his head. "Home...to Poland."

"Why?"

"I am not wanted here."

Amanda struggled to explain what he must do. "But you... you must stand up for yourself."

Jan shrugged. "Why? What does it matter whether I stand up or sit down?"

"I didn't mean literally stand up," Amanda explained, trying to reach across the barriers of language, culture, and time. "You must fight."

The young man's eyes brightened. "Fight?"

"Yes!"

Jan gazed into the distance. "My father fought for Poland. And he died."

"Then fight here in America—to become an American," Amanda said. "You have as much right to be here as anyone. You must fight for Katie. She loves you. She wants to marry you."

"But her father does not want me. I should not marry her without her father's consent."

"You can elope," Amanda said. "It would be better if he approved, but he is not a good man. This is America, Jan. It's the land of the free, and the home of the brave. Have you heard that song?"

Jan nodded. "I am brave."

"Prove it," Amanda challenged.

Throughout their conversation, Jan had closely studied Amanda's face, as if he could better understand her if he could see her words. There was a long pause, and then he shook his head, sadly. "I have already the ticket to Chicago. I will visit my brother there. Then I take the train to New York. And I take ship back to my home. Say goodbye for me. To Katie."

As he spoke, Amanda kept glancing around the waiting room. What could have happened to them? Had the deputy or the constable snatched them? Then, through the windows, she glimpsed a flash of bright color out on the platform that could only be her sister and friends.

Amanda looked at Jan. "If you insist on leaving…on *running away*…you can say goodbye to Katie yourself—to her face."

She led the young man outside where Katie and the girls had seated themselves on long, wooden bench facing the railroad tracks, which at that angle looked like silver ribbons gleaming in the moonlight.

"Katie!"

"Jan!"

In a whisper, Amanda asked Sally, "What happened to you guys?"

Her little sister said, "Some people in the station were giving us weird looks."

"We thought we'd be less conspicuous out here on the platform," Roxanne explained.

His eyebrows furrowing, Jan asked, "You look for me, Katie?"

"I'm coming *with* you," the young woman said.

"With me?"

"If you want me."

"Yes!" he said. "More than the moon and the stars."

"But we'd better hide," Amanda said, "until the train gets here."

Jan apparently had another idea. As if he had all the time in the world, he knelt on the platform, gazed up, and asked Katie, "Will you marry me?"

The girls held their breath, even as Katie promptly responded, "Yes!"

"Without your father's permission?"

"Yes!"

It appeared that a great weight had been lifted from Jan Brandowski's shoulders. He sprang to his feet and danced in a circle.

"We can live in Chicago," he said. "I will not return to Poland."

"Yes," Katie said. "I've always wanted to live in a big city, not in a town so small in mind. Away from my family. And it's no longer safe for us in Maysville."

"Then it is done," Jan Brandowski exclaimed. "We will have Polish wedding in Chicago!"

"I've heard about those Polish weddings," Amanda said. "They go on for *days.*"

"And why not?" Josie said. "As long as you're having a good time..."

Amanda still wanted to hide somewhere while they waited, but Sally announced, "Hey...the train is coming!"

Sure enough, a steaming locomotive was pulling into the station.

"I don't have a ticket!" Katie exclaimed.

"There is no time!" Jan exclaimed. "You can buy ticket on train after we board."

Katie gasped, "Oh dear, I don't have enough money. I didn't

even think…we were in such a rush…."

Jan smiled. "I have good American dollars. I will buy you ticket."

As the train wheezed to a stop and passengers began to get off, Amanda whispered to Sally, Josie, and Roxanne, "He's nice."

"Nice?" Josie snorted. "He's dreamy."

"You're boy crazy," Roxanne said.

"So?" Josie said. "Anyway, Amanda's the one with a crush on John Brandowski."

"Boys are yucky," Sally declared.

"Before long you'll be singing another tune," Josie added.

"All aboard!" the conductor called out.

"Hurry!" Amanda urged.

"Wait," Katie asked. "If Jan doesn't know you, then who *are* you?"

Not sure if she should reveal herself, Amanda hesitated. "You don't know us. We are strangers."

"From where?" Katie asked.

Amanda shook his head. "Not from where, Katie, but *when*. We don't know how or why, but we came to you from more than a hundred years in the future."

Katie laughed. "That cannot be true. You are telling a story."

Jan peered at the girls. "I believe you."

"You do?" Roxanne asked.

"I do not understand, but I feel," he explained. "I am come from a land where we are logical and, how do you say, mystical, too. We respect science, but also the mysteries of fate and destiny. Just as Copernicus proved that the earth makes an orbit of the sun, our lives are circles. We move from birth to growth to marriage, and eventually to death. And then it repeats over the generations. So maybe history, too, is not a straight line. Maybe it circles. Maybe it loops."

"I don't believe it," Roxanne scoffed.

"I will show you," Jan said. He took a lovely cameo from his shirt pocket. "This is why I came to your house tonight. To ask for your hand in marriage and make this wedding gift to you, dear Katie. It is silver, set with an amber gem, red as cherry, from the Baltics. It belonged to my great grandmother and her mother before her. The cameo has been in my family for generations. The cameo is oval, like the orbit of the earth."

"Thank you," Katie said, pinning the brooch with anxious fingers onto her blouse. "I will cherish this gift forever."

Jan turned to focus his blue eyes on Amanda. "It is a gift to one bride of each generation. Through this cameo, I show you how love spans the generations. The circle of life, and those mysterious loops in history—it is not a trick."

"Now *I* don't understand," Amanda said.

Jan shrugged. "And I know very little. Polish people suffer much, for hundreds of years, and we don't know why. Most of the universe is unknown to us. We can *see* only little pieces. How do you say, glimpses. For all that we do not know, we must have faith."

He added, "I only know that I will be good husband and father. I will work hard for my family."

As the train started to pull away from the station, everyone hugged and said goodbye. Then the young couple jumped on board.

"Thank you!" Jan called out as he and Katie waved to the four girls left on the platform.

"Yes," Katie shouted. "Thank you from the depths of my

heart." Her last words were nearly drowned out by the call of the train's steam whistle. "But what will happen to you? Will you be safe? Aren't you still—"

Before Amanda or any of the other girls could answer her, there was a clamor behind them as a gang of men burst through the doors to the platform. One of them shouted, "There they are—those gypsies who kidnapped Katie!"

"Where is my dear daughter?" Judge Blackburn shouted. "Where is she?"

"On the train!" someone exclaimed. "She's getting away!"

"Run after her!" the judge roared. "Catch her!"

VIII.

The girls suddenly found themselves in the midst of an angry mob, including Judge Clement Blackburn and Constable Calhoun.

Amanda expected the men to promptly snap handcuffs on them, but instead the judge pointed at the departing train and screamed, "Get my daughter! Now!"

However, most of the men seemed less than eager to race after the train, which was quickly picking up speed. Only Constable Calhoun hustled down the track, shouting, "Stop the train!"

Amanda recalled in that moment a family story about her great-grandfather, Old Joe. Like many poor people, he and his brother didn't have enough money for coal to heat their small apartment in Chicago. So they often walked along the railroad tracks and picked up small lumps that had fallen from passing trains. Collecting one black chunk after another, they weren't committing any crime, but a policeman had once tried to arrest them.

"We are not stealing," Joe's brother had explained. "This coal is going to waste and it is not illegal to pick it up. We're just trying to heat our homes."

"You're still vagrants," the policemen had grumbled. Pulling out two sets of handcuffs, he announced he was going to arrest them on a charge of loitering.

"Run!" Old Joe had shouted. Maybe it was wrong to run away, he always said later, but it was the only way not to be thrown in jail for picking up the fallen coal, for being poor and having no other way to stay warm.

Amanda's great-grandfather and his brother had gotten away, but now it appeared that Katie and Jan would be caught.

"Run faster, Calhoun!" Judge Blackburn ordered as the constable lumbered after the train, as if his life, or at least his job depended on it.

Amanda prayed for the locomotive to speed up, and it did, but not quite fast enough. In a last burst, Constable Calhoun lunged for the railing of the small platform at the rear of the caboose. His fingers caught hold. For a moment, he hung on, his legs churning, and then swung his left foot onto the bottom step.

"No!" screamed Amanda and Sally.

Jan Brandowski appeared in the doorway of the caboose.

The girls watched in horror as the constable clamped his right hand onto the railing. With his free hand, he was trying to pull out something. His badge? No, it was his gun!

As he did so, the train lurched. Gazing up at Jan, who resolutely stood over him, the constable struggled to hang onto the railing. But he lost his grip—or perhaps his courage—and tumbled off, rolling over and over in the gravel.

As Constable Calhoun scrambled to his feet, the train speeded up and dwindled into the night.

"They made it!" Josie exclaimed. "They got away."

"Thank God," Amanda breathed.

But now the mob tightened around them, and none of these men seemed at all pleased to have been roused from their beds so late at night.

Glancing down, Amanda gasped when she noticed the cameo brooch lying at her feet on the platform, the lovely piece of jewelry handed down in the Brandowski family over the years. It must have come unclasped as Katie and Jan hurried onto the train.

Amanda caught Josie's eye and glanced downward.

Her friend winked back at her. "Gotcha."

Josie began to jabber at the men surrounding them about their Miranda rights. She insisted they had a right to a lawyer and a phone call and a speedy trial. While the men looked at each other, bewildered, Amanda stooped down, scratched her ankle and picked up the cameo. Hiding it in her palm, she stood up again and tucked the brooch into her pocket.

Constable Calhoun stumbled back to the group, brushing himself off.

"I'm sorry, Judge," he panted. "I almost nabbed them."

Judge Blackburn scowled. "That's disappointing. But I'll just telegraph ahead to the Chicago police. When the train arrives, Central Station will be swarming with coppers! They'll arrest the boy for kidnapping my Katie and ship him right back to Maysville, where he'll be sentenced, after a fair trial of course, to spend the rest of his life in prison. Although I won't be surprised if he happens have an accident while in jail. Those things happen, you know."

Amanda stepped forward. "Jan Brandowski didn't kidnap anyone," she announced. "Your daughter eloped with him."

The judge's face pulsed red, while everyone else laughed at that outrageous claim.

"How dare you slander my daughter?" Judge Blackburn exclaimed.

"She's in love with him," Josie declared.

"Enough!" Judge Blackburn. "Slap the manacles on these gypsies and throw them in the calaboose."

"What are the charges?" the constable asked.

"Burglary," Judge Blackburn declared. "Also kidnapping. Resisting arrest. Assaulting a police officer. Attempted murder. Might as well add political agitation, too."

Judge Blackburn glanced around and addressed the crowd, "Look at how they're dressed. I've never seen such strange garments. My dear Katie would never run off with one of them."

He whirled around to confront a stout man, with a thick black cigar in the right corner of his mouth and a pen poised over a notepad in his hand. "I don't want to open the newspaper and read any of this gossip about eloping," he said to the man. "You understand, Samuel? You're the editor. It's a clear case of kidnapping. The work of gypsies and political agitators."

Puffing on the cigar, the man squinted at the girls. "They sure look like gypsies to me, Judge."

Constable Calhoun nodded to a portly man in green visor, possibly the stationmaster. "If you'd be so kind as to call for a paddy wagon, Earl, I'll have these girls locked up and out of your way, sir."

The man nodded, but didn't seem too happy about the request.

Judge Blackburn glanced at the constable. "We can escort them to the jail on foot. It will be just as fast."

"Yessir," the constable agreed, but he seemed to be having second thoughts.

As the constable stepped forward to clamp the manacles on her, Josie howled, "Don't you dare come near me!"

A man snorted, "What are you going to do about it?"

"She's crazed in the head!" another suggested.

That gave Amanda an idea.

Dangling the cameo brooch in front of her, she eyed the men ominously. "If any of you lay a hand on us, I'll cast a spell on you—a *gypsy* curse. You and your children and their children will be cursed forever."

It was an ridiculous bluff, Amanda thought, but folks must have been superstitious back then. Most of the men grew wide-eyed and took a step or two backward.

"Don't be doing anything like that, missy," one of them blubbered.

Judge Blackburn scoffed, "Don't be foolish, Elmer. She is talking nonsense."

"Am I?" Amanda intoned darkly.

A wide-eyed bystander exclaimed, "Judge, it was you who said they was gypsies!"

"But they have no real magical powers," the judge sputtered. "They are little more than liars and thieves."

While the men were mulling over these claims, Sally stepped forward.

"No magical powers?" She brandished a small, rectangular object over her head. She pointed it at the men, and suddenly, it flashed weird bright lights and made jangling noises.

She wielded the object like a weapon at the men, who sprang back in horror.

The constable sucked in a breath. "It's witchcraft!"

"Leave it to Sally to bring her Gameboy along with her," Josie whispered to the others.

"I'm surprised she didn't bring her laptop and cell phone, too," Amanda muttered.

Sally glanced at the other girls. "I do have my cell phone!" Then she touched the *Gameboy* pad, opened one of her noisiest games, and announced, "Who wants to be the first to suffer the gypsy curse?" She stepped toward one of the men.

He screeched, "She's casting spells on us!"

The men all sprang back. With a quick look at each other, and then at a freight train that was just rumbling into the station, the girls rushed through a gap and dashed across the tracks, seconds before the train rumbled past the platform.

Across the track, they could hear Judge Blackburn yelling, "After them! As soon as the train has gone by!"

But it appeared that Sally's "gypsy curse" had scared most of the men.

"I've got to get home to the missus," one of them muttered.

"It's late, Judge," another mumbled. "We'll find them easier when it's daylight."

"Cowards!" Judge Blackburn thundered as the mob melted away.

Glancing through the gaps between the passing freight cars, Amanda noticed that most of the men had drifted away. Only Judge Blackburn, Constable Calhoun, and a few rough-looking characters remained on the platform.

The girls didn't wait any longer. They ran along the tracks, south toward the underpass.

Judge Blackburn shouted into the night, "There is no way you can outrun us forever."

And Amanda knew he was right. "Somehow, we have to ditch them," she whispered to her sister and friends.

"How? Where should we go?" Josie asked.

"Back to the house," Amanda answered. "And back through the mirror, somehow."

Roxanne moaned, "Not the house again."

"Do you have any better ideas?" Amanda asked.

All they had to do was elude these men, sneak back to the house, climb to the attic, and slip back through the mirror—if they could. Amanda sensed that they *had* to do so before daybreak. If they couldn't, she feared that they would be trapped forever in 1912.

And it seemed that they had failed in their matchmaking. Jan and Katie would surely be caught at Central Station in Chicago.

Amanda had no time to think about what might happen if they couldn't elude the judge and constable. "Let's go!" she whispered.

She and the girls cut down a narrow street between two large warehouses, then hurried across Main Street where it veered under the railroad tracks. Over the years, the cluster of two-story brick warehouses in the wedge-shaped area east of the tracks had not changed much. The quaint neighborhood now housed an Italian restaurant, coffeehouse, and several fashionable shops, including Secondhand Rose, a favorite shopping destination for Amanda and her mother.

It was all so weird to Amanda, but at least she was familiar with the network of brick alleys as she steered her sister and friends along.

The girls suddenly heard Constable Calhoun bellow, "They went this way!"

He was less than half a block behind them!

Horse hooves clattered on the brick pavement.

Amanda knew they couldn't outrun him.

"Just a sec!"

She paused by one of the small warehouses and pushed open the door. Leaving it wide open, she dropped one of her dress-up scarves on the floor just inside the threshold. As she and the other girls rushed around the corner to hide in an alley next to the warehouse, Amanda snatched up a good-sized rock and flipped it to Josie. "Quick, throw it through that door!"

Josie grinned. "Sure thing."

With the fluid windup of a star pitcher, she hummed a fastball deep into the black interior of the warehouse. The stone clattered against some barrels or wooden boxes, just as the constable galloped up, followed close behind by two men on foot.

"I heard them!" the constable shouted. "In there!"

Amanda peeked around the corner.

Constable Calhoun reined in his horse, dismounted, and inspected the open doorway. "One of them lost a scarf," he announced. "They must be hiding inside."

A moment later, Judge Blackburn arrived with several other men. Short of breath, he demanded, "What's up?"

"We've got them trapped," Constable Calhoun explained. "In there."

Judge Blackburn glanced at the doorway. "Why would they leave the door open?" he growled.

"They were in a hurry," the constable pointed out. "And they dropped a scarf, too."

"Clearly a trick," the judge said.

The men argued for a moment. The judge looked around the narrow streets, and Amanda quickly ducked back. A moment later, she peeked out again.

To her shock and dismay, she saw an amazing sight. As the two men continued to squabble, a stumpy old beagle sauntered past them to the warehouse door.

"Tulip!" Sally gasped from behind Amanda. All the girls crowded around Amanda, straining to see what was going on.

"Where the heck did she come from?" Josie asked.

Roxanne whispered, "And what's she doing?"

Amanda sighed. "Search me."

The girls watched as the Regal Beagle waddled through the men's legs and sat down in the doorway.

Constable Calhoun exclaimed, "See, Judge? Their stupid dog is following their scent. It's leading us right to them."

The judge snickered. "You're right. Okay, men, tear the warehouse apart—shoot anything that moves, including that fat little dog."

Tulip gazed up at Judge Blackburn, as if hanging on his every word. Then, with a leisurely yawn, she struggled to her feet and moseyed inside, pushing her grizzled nose against the door. With a loud clank, it swung closed.

"Hey!" one of the men shouted.

The constable rushed forward and tried the door. "The dog locked us out!"

The judge snapped at him, "That mutt is smarter than you. It's smarter than all of you idiots put together."

No one looked pleased by that snide remark.

The judge grumbled, "Don't just stand there. Batter down the door!"

Taking turns, with *oofs* and cries of pain, the men futilely pounded their shoulders against the thick, solidly-built door.

"Let's go," Amanda said.

"But what about Tulip?" Sally asked.

Amanda hated to abandon their little dog, but knew there was nothing they could do with all those men out on the street. "We need to go. Tulip's giving us a chance to get away."

"Maybe she knows what she's doing," Josie added. "She's smarter than she looks. Besides—"

She was interrupted by a soft *screech* overhead.

The girls looked up, just as the metal cover of an air vent creaked open.

A moment later Tulip squeezed her bulk through the small rectangular hole. Then she jumped, her floppy ears spread like wings, as if she were Super Dog. Instinctively, Amanda caught the dog, tumbling on the brick pavement under the weight of the hefty hound.

The girls hugged Tulip and whispered their thanks.

Meanwhile, the men around the corner continued to slam themselves against the sturdy door.

"We need a crowbar, sir," one of the men suggested, but the door was already splintering. With one last shove, the wood around the lock gave way and the door flew open.

"After them!" the judge shouted.

The men rushed into the warehouse.

Given a fresh headstart, the girls threaded their way through the narrow alleys between the brick buildings until they came to

First Street on the east side of the warehouse district.

They hesitated in the shadows by a brick wall.

In the present day, the four-lane thoroughfare was busy, with lots of traffic. Now, late at night, it was hauntingly deserted, but still brightly lit with streetlamps.

The girls glanced both ways and rushed across that wide stretch of open pavement. At any moment Amanda expected a shout: "There they are!"

But they made it to the other side, unnoticed, and hustled into a quiet neighborhood of thick bushes, trees, and small clapboard houses. It felt good to have a little cover, but it didn't feel safe anywhere.

It was so quiet, even for Maysville. Eerily quiet. Someone might be lurking in the shadows, waiting to ambush them.

Wide-eyed, the girls walked along quickly.

Occasionally glancing over their shoulders, they zigzagged down streets and alleys, hoping to shake any pursuers who were not back at the warehouse.

As the girls hurried down a dark alley, Josie dared to whisper, "Hey, what about your dog, Amanda?"

Tulip had waddled along with the girls for about ten feet, but once again, she had vanished.

Amanda sighed. "I guess she couldn't keep up."

"It was cool how she fooled those dopes," Josie said.

"She *must* have come to look out for us," Amanda reasoned. "I'm gonna to have to start giving that old dog more credit."

In a soft voice, Sally said, "We can't leave without Tulip."

"We can wait for her back at the house," Amanda said. "I'm sure she'll catch up."

Sally didn't appear convinced.

Moments later, however, a fat little dog rocketed past them.

Josie's mouth dropped open. "I've never seen that dog move so fast. Come to think of it, I've never seen her move much at all."

"Maybe she's helping us again," Roxanne suggested brightly.

Tulip had indeed turned out to be a heroic hound, but Amanda smiled to herself. "More likely Tulip wants to make sure we don't leave her behind."

The girls enjoyed a joyful moment until Josie suggested, "Hey, as long as we're here, why don't we hang around town for a few days? Then pop back through the mirror. We could sure do one heck of a school report about what we saw. You know, what we did on our summer vacation."

Amanda would have liked to explore the past of her hometown, but in a safe and leisurely fashion. "You don't think we'd be noticed or anything?" she pointed out.

"We could buy new clothes and dress like ladies," Josie suggested.

"*You* dressed like a lady?" Amanda exclaimed. "That'll be the day."

"Let's just go home," Roxanne pleaded. "Please."

"Yes," Sally said in a small voice. "I miss Mom."

Josie persisted, "With new clothes and a little makeup, we won't stick out like sore thumbs."

"Knock it off," Roxanne groaned. "By tomorrow there will be Wanted posters for us all around town."

"And we may have only one chance to go back through the mirror," Amanda said. "I've got a strange feeling—don't ask me to explain it—that by morning, the mirror will lose its magic. I'm not even sure we can still go back tonight."

Roxanne gasped. "Don't say that."

"And what if that Judge Blackburn gets suspicious about the mirror and shatters it?" Josie added calmly.

"Don't say that!"

They were soon approaching their neighborhood. It was so quiet and charming with the misty streetlamps, ornate hitching posts, and brick sidewalks and streets. But the calm frightened Amanda. Many of the men had gone home, but Judge Clement Blackburn and Constable Calhoun would never abandon the hunt. And they must be furious about the little trick at the empty warehouse. Could those two men and a few of their cohorts be lurking somewhere in the shadows now?

As the girls came to the northwest corner of the park, however, Amanda began to take heart. They were so close. And no one would think that they would return to the house. They slipped into Ellsworth Park and crept from one clump of bushes to another.

"Hopefully, Mrs. Blackburn and that snot-nosed brat Orville have gone to sleep," Amanda said. "We'll sneak into the house and upstairs to the attic."

"What if they're *not* asleep?" Roxanne whispered. "And what if the doors are locked?"

"People never locked their doors back then," Josie pointed out.

"But they might tonight—after everything that's happened," Roxanne said.

"Then we'll sneak in through a window," Sally suggested.

It was a warm summer night. Amanda couldn't imagine that the Blackburns would close their upstairs windows. The girls could surely climb one of the downspouts or a lattice to one of the second-floor porches of the Victorian house.

As the girls came to the house, they hurried across the street to the hedge along the west side, as they had earlier in the night.

"No one in sight," Josie whispered.

"What about Tulip?" Sally asked again. "You said we'd wait for her."

"It's late and we can't stay long," Amanda said, glancing at the sky. It was very dark, but she remembered the saying, *It's always darkest just before dawn.*

"We don't have much time left," she whispered. "It's almost sunrise."

Nonetheless the four girls lingered in the bushes. The minutes went by agonizingly.

Finally Roxanne whispered, "You know, Sally, your dog *is* old. She's enjoyed a good, long life."

Josie snorted, "If you call sleeping and eating 'a good life.'"

Amanda perked up. "Eating?"

"What?" Roxanne asked.

"I've got a hunch where we might find Tulip," Amanda muttered.

"Where?" Roxanne asked.

"Follow me."

The girls crept along the hedge to the backyard, then hustled across the lawn.

"The smokehouse?" Josie asked.

"Where else?" Amanda said.

The door was ajar.

The interior glistened black from all the smoke, but there was enough moonlight for the girls to see the Regal Beagle squatting on the floor—in the midst of a pile of half-eaten cured hams, slabs of bacon, and rings of sausage.

Tulip glanced up nonchalantly, and then resumed gnawing with abandon on a hambone.

"How could you?" Amanda scolded.

The dog paused to gaze sad-eyed at her.

"Don't give me that look," Amanda groaned.

"She did help us," Roxanne said.

"And she must have worked up quite an appetite," Josie added.

"Yeah, for the first time in her life," Sally said.

Tulip released a long sigh, as if she couldn't eat another bit. Nonetheless, a second later she reconsidered and sank her teeth into a smoked sausage.

"Now I know why you were in such a hurry to get back here," Sally said.

Amanda urged, "Now let's just *go*, Tulip. We've got to hurry."

"Come on, Tulip," Sally said. "Good dog."

The plump dog gazed longingly at all the smoked meat piled around her. It was obvious that she did not want to abandon such a feast.

Amanda promised her, "We'll prepare a banquet for you, Tulip, when we get back."

The old dog sighed and staggered to her feet. With her bloated belly, Tulip could barely stand up, let alone creep forward. She tottered on her short legs.

"We'll have to carry her," Josie groaned.

"She's too heavy," Amanda said.

The girls helped the stuffed mutt down the wooden steps and into the yard. She lumbered along, her pink belly scraping the ground, as the girls crept up to the house and tiptoed up the creaky wooden steps. The floorboards ached beneath their feet as the girls crossed the porch. Ever so carefully, Josie tried the screen door—it was unlocked.

Amanda was suspicious.

Easing the screen door open, the girls slipped through the kitchen and dining room, and into parlor. They turned toward the stairs, just as a shadow swept over them.

IX.

Behind them a voice boomed. "Halt! Or I'll shoot!"
The girls whirled around. There stood Constable Calhoun, blocking the doorway back into the dining room. He pointed the double-barrels of a shotgun at their faces.

Clutching his own shotgun, the Honorable Judge Clement Blackburn eased from the shadows near the front door. "I thought you might come sneaking back here for some foolish reason or other. To *steal* clothes and jewelry from my daughter—or maybe take that mirror which is so precious to her," he said. "Why else would you have been up in the attic in the first place?"

Armed with her hand ax, Mabel Blackburn then emerged from the shadows in the doorway to the study. To complete the picture, little Orville appeared alongside her with that malicious smirk—so like his father.

"Turn on the porch light, Orville," Judge Blackburn ordered, "while I keep a bead on the miscreants."

His son gleefully skipped over to the front door and complied.

"That's the signal." The judge peered at the girls with an

evil gleam in his eyes. "My posse—what's left of it—has been hiding in the neighborhood. As I speak, they are tightening the noose around the house."

The girls went limp, which prompted the judge to chortle, "There's no escape this time! You're trapped like rats."

As the other men sifted into the house, they filled every doorway and window.

But no one had bothered with the stairway. The girls could race up to the attic, Amanda thought, and hopefully go right through the mirror, if they were fast enough. But what about Tulip? She could never keep up with them.

And where had she gone now? Amanda wondered.

As if on cue, the little dog ambled right past the constable's feet and into the parlor. She paused to look at everyone, yawned as if she didn't have a care in the world, and started up the stairs as if she owned the place.

"What's that mongrel doing?" Judge Blackburn raged. He nodded at the dog, but kept his shotgun fixed on the girls.

As Tulip struggled up each step, the pudgy mutt glanced back at the girls. Amanda could swear that the little beagle winked at her.

Suddenly Amanda had an idea. Turning back to the judge, she said, "Okay, you've caught us redhanded, but we have to go up to the attic."

The judge peered suspiciously at the girls, as Tulip continued to labor up the stairs. "Why?"

Looking puzzled, Mrs. Blackburn noted, "That's where I first heard the girls, Clement. Maybe the dog has come back for something they left up there."

The judge snorted, "Maybe its favorite bone."

"Or something dangerous!" Mabel Blackburn exclaimed.

Constable Calhoun was alarmed. "What's in the attic?" he demanded, waving the shotgun at them. "Do you have a *bomb* up there? Are you anarchists? Agitators?"

Amanda fumbled for an excuse. "Uh, we simply left all our belongings there!"

"Belongings?" the judge asked. "What were you doing in our attic in the first place?"

"It's a long story."

Amanda hoped to stall the men long enough for Tulip to mount the stairs to the attic, but that might take the rest of the night. Having gorged in the smokehouse, the dog had managed to climb a few steps and then, wheezing heavily, she had to rest for a while. Pink tongue hanging out, she drooled on the polished oak tread, only halfway up the stairs.

Although very anxious, Constable Calhoun stepped forward. "Don't worry, Judge, I'll kick their dog down the stairs and fetch the wenches' rags from the attic."

Amanda gasped, "Oh no! You can't do that!"

Judge Blackburn squinted at Amanda. "Young lady, you are in no position to negotiate *anything*. I give the orders around here!"

For emphasis, he cocked both barrels of his shotgun. It's all over, Amanda thought.

At that moment, Tulip resumed her climb with vigor.

Josie chuckled. "Look at Tulip go!"

Orville shouted, "Catch the dog! I want to keep it!" In knickers and Buster Brown shoes, he rushed over to his father and clutched at his arm. "Can't I keep the dog? You never let me have a pet."

Judge Blackburn snapped. "No! I'm not feeding that gluttonous mutt. Just think how much that fat little beast would eat."

"No!" Mabel Blackburn added. "Orville, dear, think of the mess it would make in the house!"

Overcome with fury, Orville kicked at his father with his clunky shoes and ranted, "I hate you! I hate you! I hate you!"

"Run!" Amanda cried out, as if the girls needed a hint.

"Out of the way, boy!" Judge Blackburn ordered, wildly swinging his shotgun. "I can't get a clear shot!"

Sally was already scrambling toward the stairs, with Roxanne and Josie hard on her heels. Amanda raced after them, just as twin blasts of the shotgun rumbled through the house.

She winced as bits of plaster exploded around her, but felt no pain, not in her arms, legs, or back. The cross-eyed weasel missed me, she thought, unless in her shock she hadn't yet felt the sting of the pellets.

"Oh my God!" Mabel Blackburn shrieked.

As she tore up the stairs, Amanda glanced back.

Orville Blackburn lay crumpled to the floor.

Judge Blackburn sagged to his knees and dropped the shotgun, which clattered on the polished floor.

Mabel Blackburn cried, "You've killed our dear sweet boy!"

Judge Blackburn shouted after the girls, "It's all their fault! After them, Calhoun!"

"Tend to your boy," the constable said. "I'll catch them, sir!"

Amanda rushed in a panic after the other girls, the clump of heavy feet right behind her.

She whirled around the second-floor landing and scrambled up the narrow staircase that led to the attic, right behind her friends and sister.

"Hurry!" Roxanne called back.

Amanda got to the top of the stairs, but it was too late. Just before she reached the last step, she felt the hot breath of her pursuer on her neck.

In that instant, Constable Calhoun lunged and clamped a meaty hand onto the girl's ankle.

"Got you!"

Amanda struggled to break away, but it was hopeless. The constable was a powerful man, and he had a firm grip on her ankle.

Having been passed by everyone as she labored up the stairs, Tulip finally caught up with Constable Calhoun. The little dog promptly sank her teeth into the man's leg.

Yow!" howled the constable, as he struggled to hold onto Amanda's ankle and pull her down.

Amanda kicked at him with her free leg, but the constable only tightened his grip. "Go on without me!" she called to the other girls.

"No way," Josie said, scrambling back. With a rebel yell, she cocked her leg back and aimed a soccer kick at the side of the constable's head.

The heavy man grunted and let go of Amanda's ankle as he tumbled back down the steep attic stairs.

On his way, he crashed into Judge Blackburn who was coming up, and the two of them landed in a tangled heap at the foot of the stairs.

"You oaf," the judge hollered.

"I had one of them—but that dog bit me! And then one of the girls kicked me! I'm injured."

The judge seethed. "Your pain is the least of my worries.

Get after those girls!"

"I almost broke my neck!" the constable groaned.

"I'll have your neck if you let any of those girls get away. There is no escape from the attic. The fools have trapped themselves."

"Sir, what about your son? Shouldn't you be tending to him?"

Judge Blackburn yelled, "Not now! After them!"

In the attic above, Amanda was shocked. Could the man be so obsessed with his own pride that he would abandon his dying son?

"Come on, Amanda!" Josie urged. Together, the four girls panicked as they heard footsteps pounding up the stairs.

Thankfully, the mirror still stood in the middle of the room.

"Let's go!" Josie yelled.

But Sally hesitated. "Where's Tulip?"

Amanda sputtered, "Back on the stairs, but she'll be coming."

"Promise?"

"Yes!"

Sally lowered her shoulder, just like she'd played football with their dad when she was little. With reckless abandon, she would run the length of the living room to crash into him as he sat on the carpet, and topple him, again and again. Now, she raced at the glass oval mirror on its sturdy wooden frame at full speed.

Amanda expected the mirror to shatter when her sister blasted against it. But to her delight, Sally vanished through the polished silvery surface, as if plunging into a pool of water.

Josie and Roxanne took heart and rushed to follow the little roustabout. Like Sally, the two girls disappeared through the mirror.

Amanda felt suddenly alone. She waited just a moment, hoping to see Tulip pulling herself up the last step and plodding into the attic.

But instead, the husky form of Constable Calhoun darkened the doorway.

"It's all over, girlie."

But Amanda could only think of Tulip. Was she still struggling up the stairs? Or had she foolishly doubled-back and headed to the smokehouse for another late-night snack?

"Where are your friends hiding?" the constable demanded as he eased into the attic, with the judge right behind him. Both of them were catching their breath, their faces red with exertion.

"They're gone!" Amanda shouted. "And you'll never find them."

"We saw all of you run into the attic," the judge snarled. "Guard the door, Calhoun. These girls aren't going anywhere."

"Be careful, Judge. They were so desperate to get to the attic," the constable said. "They may have come to fetch a bomb."

As the judge rummaged through the boxes and trunks, he called out, "May as well give yourself up, girls. You can't hide up here, not for long."

Mrs. Blackburn puffed up the stairs. "The boy's hurt bad, Clement!" she cried out.

"We'll fetch the doctor," Judge Blackburn said. "By and by."

"I have called him, but I fear the worst. Orville is bleeding out; he may die. Wouldn't you like a last word with him?" Her voice was hysterical, on the edge of breaking.

The judge waved her off. "The boy will be fine. Guard the door, Mabel, so this lout can help me flush out those other girls."

Uncertain what to do, the woman filled the doorway, folding

her arms and planting her legs. "But Clement…"

"Hush," the judge dismissed her.

The two men inspected every nook and cranny, box by box, trunk by trunk, but they found no trace of the girls anywhere in the attic.

Judge Blackburn was puzzled. "They couldn't have squeezed through the tiny windows. They're too small, even for those scrawny girls."

Mouth hung open, the constable was aghast. "They've vanished into thin air."

Mrs. Blackburn exclaimed nervously, "They really must be gypsies. They used their black magic!"

"Hogwash," the judge grumbled.

They might have stood there bewildered for the rest of the night, had not Mabel Blackburn shrieked, "Egad, something is scurrying up my leg!"

The constable shrugged. "Probably just a rat."

"A rat!" the woman hiked up her skirts and did a little jig, while—to Amanda's delight—Tulip, calm as can be, sauntered between the lady's ample legs.

As if she hadn't a care in the world, the little dog loped over to Amanda, sat down on her haunches, and yawned again.

"That beagle!" the woman growled. "It's time she had her day of reckoning."

"Don't touch my dog!" Amanda cried out. She hoisted Tulip into her arms, staggering under the load.

"Careful," the constable cautioned Mrs. Blackburn. "It may be the dog that has the black magic."

Amanda threw a sly, knowing look at the man. "And Tulip just might make *you* vanish into thin air," she warned, pointing the beagle, nose first, at the lady, as if Tulip were a magician's wand. Amanda couldn't aim the hefty dog for very long, but the ruse worked.

Mrs. Blackburn and the constable cringed. "Enough of your nonsense," the judge grumbled, but he too kept his distance and merely asked, "Where are your friends hiding?"

"Far away from here," Amanda said. "In time. Not in place."

"She's speaking in riddles!" Mrs. Blackburn gasped.

"Please, young lady, don't work any of your black magic on us," the constable begged. He squirmed, as if ready to run for his life.

Amanda eased toward the mirror.

"Just where do you think you're going, missy?" the judge demanded.

"Uh...I'm going to fix my hair." Amanda paused in front of the mirror.

"Fiddlesticks!" Mrs. Blackburn harped.

"What's the point of that, you foolish girl," the judge said in a mocking tone. "You and your friends will never get away."

"It really would seem impossible," Amanda agreed. "Unless..."

With Tulip in her arms, she carefully took a step into the mirror. Her leg disappeared up to her hip. She lifted her other leg over the frame of the mirror and stepped fully into the silvery surface. Amanda tarried long enough to observe the look of shock and terror on the faces of her pursuers.

Then, she and Tulip plunged through the mirror, into a black realm of no light in which she was as light as air, unable to touch anything.

As if far, far way, Amanda heard Mabel Blackburn caterwaul,

"She vanished, Clement—right through that mirror!"

Amanda could hear, faintly, Judge Blackburn yelling, "Go after them, Calhoun!"

"I ain't going near that mirror!" Constable Calhoun sputtered. "It's witchcraft!"

To her horror, Amanda heard the judge, in a distant whisper: "Then I'll go after them."

Amanda and Tulip broke into an amazing brilliance and tumbled onto the plank floor of the attic. The other girls rushed up to her. "You made it, Amanda!"

Thankfully, the four girls were back in the attic in their own time, safe and sound—until the mirror vibrated.

Amanda blurted, "Hurry! The judge is coming after us. We have to get out of the attic!"

But it was too late. They heard a rumble and voices on the other side.

"Oh no!" Roxanne cried.

All the girls tingled with fear. They should have fled downstairs, but gathered around the mirror, frozen with terror.

Then—

"Dagnabbit! I cannot pass through the mirror!" Judge Blackburn thundered. "The fool thing won't let me. Maybe you'll have better luck, Calhoun."

"Me?" the constable squeaked.

A pause, then the constable mumbled in a thin, reluctant voice, "Okay, I'll give it a try while you tend to the missus, Judge. I do believe she's fainted."

For a moment there was silence on the other side of the mirror. The girls tensed, until they heard another "Dagnabbit!"

This one was even louder, and the mirror seemed to tremble with an impact. But to the girls' relief no one appeared through it.

Judge Blackburn asked in a shaky voice, "What happened, Amos?"

In a dazed voice, the constable answered, "For the love of God, I don't know, sir. I'm gobsmacked."

"Gobsmacked." It was the last word that the girls ever heard through the mirror. Later, it would become a little joke among them. But now they collapsed in a heap among the dress-up clothes strewn around them.

Roxanne exhaled, "Whew, I cannot believe we actually made it back. It feels like we've been up all night."

"We have been up all night," Josie pointed out.

Indeed they could see that dawn was breaking outside the windows.

"We made it back just in time," Amanda said.

The girls were overjoyed.

Then the mirror vibrated again.

"Oh no!" Roxanne cried. "They haven't given up! They're still coming after us!"

Instinctively, the girls looked around for weapons. Sally had already grabbed one of her old baseball bats.

They all held their breaths as they watched the mirror for what seemed like hours, though it was no more than a few seconds. Then the mirror became still. For a moment, the girls stared at it, afraid to blink. Then Amanda raised her hand.

"Don't touch it!" Roxanne exclaimed.

Amanda eased her palm forward, let her fingertips touch the mirror. It was cold, hard glass. She pushed against it, but the mirror was impenetrable.

A smile brightened her face. "We can't go back," Amanda said, thankful for once for something that she could not do. "And no one can come after us—I hope."

"Maybe we should break the mirror," Josie suggested. "Just to be sure."

"That's seven years' bad luck," Roxanne said. "We've had enough bad luck for one night."

"What do you mean?" Josie countered. "We all got through it and back—without a scratch."

"But we didn't accomplish anything," Roxanne argued. "The police must have caught Katie and Jan in Chicago. We probably made things worse for them, and almost got ourselves killed in the process. Like they say, 'No good deed goes unpunished.'"

"We'll see," Amanda said. "We still have some investigating to do."

"Oh no," Roxanne groaned. "Count me out, Amanda. This was supposed to be a *sleep*over. And that's what we should have been doing. It's one thing to stay up late on purpose—and another to be kept up all night running for our lives."

"But Tulip saved us!" Sally exclaimed.

Josie snorted. "Hard to believe."

Amanda gazed adoringly at their grizzled beagle. She had always admired the loyalty and hard work of those heroic dogs who rescued children and assisted people with disabilities. Tulip, however, had always thought only of her own appetites and comforts—until last night, when she had risen to the occasion.

Sally sighed, "Tulip would have given her life to save us, if she had to."

"Or worse, that brat Orville would have adopted her," Josie said.

Roxanne agreed, "That would have been a fate worse than death."

Squatting on the bare boards of the attic floor, Tulip yawned, as though bored.

"But we all love Tulip," Josie said, and the four girls bent down, and lavished pets and hugs on the little dog.

Her Highness the Hound did her best to ignore them as she struggled to her feet, hoisted her nose, and waddled toward the door.

Amanda called after her. "Where are you going, Tulip?"

"Downstairs," Josie chuckled. "To mooch another snack in the kitchen."

Amanda sighed, "She's probably going to take a nap. I can't imagine anyone, even her, eating any more food tonight."

"I could use a little shut-eye myself," Josie said.

"Great idea!" Roxanne agreed. "Let's go down and get into our sleeping bags."

"Too much trouble," Josie muttered.

Exhausted, they sprawled on the soft piles of dress-up clothes.

They were just drifting into the sweetest sleep imaginable when the doorbell rang downstairs. Tulip went berserk, which was very strange. Their old beagle rarely went to the effort of barking at anyone. And when she did, she annoyed everyone in the family, because she only barked at friendly people like the mail carrier or paperboy. They doubted if she'd ever bother with a burglar.

So it couldn't be anyone threatening, Amanda concluded and the beagle yaps were music to her ears.

Then again, the sun was just rising over the ragged trees. Who could be calling at such an early hour?

Curious, the girls roused themselves and crept down the stairs to the second floor.

"What the heck?" Amanda's father growled, knotting his bathrobe, as he stumbled blurry-eyed out of the bedroom. He looked surprised to see the girls.

"You up already?" he asked.

The girls glanced at each other.

"Um, we've been up for a while," Josie said.

"Oh yeah," Amanda's father joked. "It was a sleepover, which means you girls didn't sleep much, right?"

Amanda confessed that they had been up *all* night.

"All night?" Mr. Tucker chuckled.

Amanda shrugged. "It's a long story, Dad."

Once again the doorbell rang.

"Who could be coming here at daybreak?" he wondered aloud.

Before anyone could think of a likely answer, the doorbell *burred* again—a long, persistent ring.

Tulip began to howl.

"This had better be important," Amanda's dad muttered.

Liddy Tucker ambled out of the bedroom. "Who could be bothering us at this ungodly hour—and what are you girls doing up so early?"

Again the four girls looked at each other.

The Tucker parents stumbled down the stairs to the front door, and the girls trailed after them.

In the kitchen, Tulip continued to howl over her food dish until Steven Tucker opened the front door, then the old dog went silent. She didn't even resume chowing down.

An old man with a cane swept into the hallway and immediately demanded, "I've come for the mirror! I must have that mirror! I will pay any price!"

Despite his aged face, Amanda was shocked to recognize none other than the boy she had last seen lying crumpled on the floor of a hallway—Orville Blackburn!

"You?" Liddy Tucker asked as she tightened the knot in her bathrobe. "The old man from the auction. What are *you* doing here?"

"My grandparents told me how those girls had passed through the mirror—that they must have come back in time," the old man prattled on.

His eyes were wild. "If my grandparents had shattered the mirror, they might have undone those dreadful events. But Grandmama was terrified of the evil mirror. She didn't want it in the house, and had someone carry it away. Only later, long after Aunt Katie had run away, did Grandpapa realize that there might still be time, since the girls had come from the distant future. All their lives, my grandparents and father searched for the mirror—in hopes that he could destroy it before those girls found it."

Creeping farther down the stairs, Amanda spoke softly, "You're not Orville. You're his son!"

The old man removed his hat and nodded. "Orville Blackburn, Junior."

"It's too late," Amanda told him. "It was done—last night."

In a bare whisper, the old man muttered, "No, it cannot be.

I was so close on the trail of the mirror. You see, Grandmama was so terrified of the cursed object that she didn't want it in the house. She sold the mirror to a curiosity shop, but then Grandfather came to think ironically that the only way to bring good luck to the family was to break the mirror. But somebody else had already bought the mirror. And then…" He hesitated as he peered at Amanda, her sister, and friends. "*You* are the girls who broke into our house."

"Not really," Amanda said, "since it's our house now—and was when we went through the mirror."

"You live here?" he asked. "In my grandparents' old house?"

"Yep," Sally said, leaning forward, fists clenched, in her brawler stance. "It's *our* home."

The old man gazed around the house and muttered as if speaking to himself, "I should have known that the mirror would come full circle—back to this house. My grandfather had placed the house in a trust, and when he passed away, my parents inherited the family home. But when they died, I could not afford the upkeep for such a big house and it stood empty for a few years—until the trust funds were exhausted. It was sold for back taxes."

Josie was in awe. "So your father—Orville Senior—didn't die when his father—your grandfather—shot him."

"Who shot who?" Liddy Tucker gasped. "Just what is going on, girls?"

"We'll tell you later, Mom," Amanda said. "After you've had your coffee."

"I must have the mirror," the old man insisted.

"You can't," Amanda told the old man. "It's ours now. Like this house. Besides, the mirror isn't magic anymore. After we returned through it last night, it changed back into an ordinary piece of furniture."

Amanda's mother and father didn't know what to say. They just stood their with their mouths slightly open, trying to figure out what the girls and the old geezer were talking about.

"But I must try," the old man pleaded. "My grandparents and my father, God rest their souls, knew I would never give up if there was a chance to try to fix history."

He looked desperate. "You destroyed our family. Katie went away forever. My grandparents and father never got over it. And my grandfather couldn't live down the dreadful shooting of his own son. Of course he never became mayor. Everyone in town was leery of him, and our family lived as social outcasts. And now I'll never be able to make it different."

Josie asked, "The police didn't arrest Jan when he and Katie got to Chicago?"

The old man scowled. "Jan was far smarter than my grandfather. He and Katie got off at a station on the Southside, close to his brother's home, not far from the meat-packing companies on Halsted Street. It never occurred to my grandfather, of course, that they would not journey all the way downtown to Central Station, which was then the main passenger terminal for the Illinois Central Railroad."

"You mean those two got married?" Roxanne exclaimed.

Hat in hand, Junior Blackburn bowed his head. "Yes."

"Wow," Sally said. "Just like in a fairy tale."

Amanda smiled. "You can say that again, little sister."

Until then, she hadn't been sure why the Tucker girls and their friends had become entangled in this drama. The girls had gone back to ensure that the right events had occurred. Jan and

Katie had needed their help to escape the clutches of Katie's father, Judge Blackburn. If she hadn't stepped through the mirror, and if the other girls hadn't followed...

As with everything in life, so much happened by chance.

Or was it destiny, as Jan believed? Was there some great circle of time, instead of a straight line from yesterday to today to tomorrow?

"None of them ever saw Katie and her family again," Junior confessed. "For years, they lived in Chicago and often invited us to their home, but Grandpapa would never allow it. Even at Thanksgiving and Christmas. He disowned her."

"You and your father never went to visit on your own?" Josie asked.

The old man shook his head. "Grandpapa told folks in town that Katie had been kidnapped and murdered by criminals that he had heroically managed to run out of town. He even had a gravestone with Katie's name on it set up in Roselawn Cemetery. He hoped to gain sympathy in the mayoral election, but everyone had turned against him. They whispered that he was an evil man for mistreating an innocent boy and chasing away his own daughter. It was terrible gossip that ruined his reputation for as long as he lived."

"So there always were good people in Maysville," Amanda said. "Even back then."

Junior rambled on, "Grandpapa was a broken man. Eventually, Jan and Katie even moved back to Maysville. But he would never allow any of us to visit their family. He still blamed them for his failure."

Josie snorted. "Sounds like him."

"Your father should have run away from his parents, like Katie did," Josie counseled. "He shouldn't have spent his whole life chasing a lost cause and made you do the same."

"Yes," Junior admitted. "And I did want to visit Katie and Jan's family. I was an only child and quite lonely. I grew up with only one mission in life—to find and shatter that mirror. It had ruined three generations of our family. Our only hope, my grandfather and father came to believe, was to find the mirror again after my grandmother sold it and it disappeared."

"So they poisoned you with their own hate," Amanda said.

"I never hated them," Junior reflected. "How could I? I never even knew them."

"Didn't you ever get married and have your own family?" Roxanne asked.

"No," the old man said, lowering his head. "Father arranged a marriage for my father, Orville Senior, to a young lady who was orphaned and in great need of a husband. No one in town would ever have allowed a daughter to marry into the Blackburn family. But it was not a happy marriage. Father never loved Mother and often treated her badly. Alas, I never found a girl who would have me, at least a proper lady of whom my grandparents and father approved."

"What a sad story," Roxanne said.

"Tragic," Josie said. "But that crazy judge deserved what he got. For beating Jan and trying to run Katie's life. And chasing us all over town."

"I always tried to be a good boy," Orville Junior said, hanging his head. "Now I'm an old man and more alone than ever. Everyone is dead now—Grandpapa, Grand-mama, Father, Katie, Jan...."

"Why wasn't your father killed dead?" Sally asked point-blank. "When your grandfather shot him?"

"He was terribly wounded by the shotgun pellets," the old man said. "He almost bled to death while Grandpapa pursued you. Luckily, the doctor arrived in time and rushed him to the hospital."

"What an awful man that judge was," Josie exclaimed. "And his wife, too. Your grandparents almost let your father die, just so they could keep their daughter from running away with the man she loved."

Junior Blackburn stared at the floor. "I know that Jan proved to be a good husband, father, and provider. He became a respected businessman. He and Katie's children all went to college and on to fine careers. They truly lived the American dream."

Mr. and Mrs. Tucker stood there, bewildered, as this unbelievable story was recounted.

"Your father…was shot by your grandfather?" Steven Tucker inquired.

"He nearly…bled to death?" Liddy Tucker asked.

"And you girls…know all about it?" their father asked, looking in amazement at Amanda and Sally.

The sisters looked sideways at each other.

"Uh, we were kind of there," Amanda said.

Mrs. Tucker shook her head in disbelief. "Would you please explain what is going on here?"

"We will," Amanda said, glancing at her sister and friends. "But you'd better sit down, Mom. You too, Dad."

However, before she could start to tell about the strange events of that night, Tulip ambled through the dining room, after pausing in the doorway to sniff at Orville Junior. Then, she continued on her path to a favorite spot to take a long nap.

"Your dog?" Orville Blackburn Junior exclaimed. "Is this the same little dog that I heard journeyed with you through the mirror?"

"Yes," Amanda said.

The old man sighed. "I always longed to have a dog. But my father forbid me to have any pet, even a parakeet. Mother said that a dog would be too much work and Father never liked animals. But he often talked, with a fond, faraway look in his eyes, about a fat little beagle that he once had hoped to have as a loving companion."

Amanda was sorry to hear yet another sad story of the old man's life.

Orville Junior licked his lips. "I must ask. What will you do with the mirror?"

"It belongs here," Amanda said. "It's part of the history of this house."

"May I at least look at it?"

Amanda shook her head. "You should go visit your family instead. You must have nieces and nephews from Katie and Jan Brandowski's descendants. Maybe you can buy them a pet. A beagle. Or at least a parakeet."

A sliver of a smile brightened the old man's face. "I think I will."

It appeared that he was about to leave when he hesitated, fingering the brim of his hat, as if struggling with a sudden realization. "After searching for the mirror for so long, I must tell you that I always knew it was a fool's errand, born of nothing but hatred and intolerance. Instead, I could have made more of my life."

He looked down at his shoes. "And I feel that I must apologize to you. I am sorry for the conduct of my grandparents, father, and…"

He glanced at Liddy Tucker. "…and recently of myself. I was quite rude to you at the auction. I believe I made an unpleasant scene." He bowed low.

As he stepped back, he looked back at the girls. "And I would like to thank you. Thank you, young ladies, for lifting a burden from an old man's heart."

Without another word, Orville Blackburn Junior walked out the door.

Epilogue

Amanda and Sally's parents weren't sure what to make of the girls' story, especially when the mirror no longer had its magic, which of course they immediately checked again. All of them marched up to the attic, carefully touched the silver surface, and then knocked on the mirror, front and back, and all around the wooden frame.

They had to admit that the old man—the grandson of Clement and Mabel Blackburn—had been so sincere when he poured out his sad story. Of course the odd tale had been confirmed in all its details, in a rush of chatter from all four girls, after Orville Junior left.

"No more late-night adventures," Liddy Tucker scolded.

Amanda rolled her eyes. "You don't have to worry about that, Mom."

Mrs. Tucker also protested when the girls cooked up a big breakfast buffet as a thank-you for Tulip. "That dog is supposed to be on a diet!"

"Trust me, Mom," Amanda said. "Tulip actually got plenty of exercise last night."

"That is the most unbelievable part of the story," Steven Tucker quipped.

"But she also cleaned out the smokehouse," Sally said.

"Now, *that* I do believe," their father said.

Given all the ham and sausage the grizzled beagle had gobbled last night, Amanda was surprised the old dog still had an appetite or any room in her belly for more food: a dozen fried eggs, a whole slab of bacon, a package of boiled hot dogs (one of her favorite snacks)—and even a ring of *kielbasa* sausage, in honor of Jan Brandowski's Polish heritage.

Later that morning, Roxanne went home—actually rushed out the door—vowing never to have another sleepover with Amanda.

After she and Josie had left, Sally piped up, "From now on, I'm sticking with computers and sports. Even football is a lot safer than going back in time." She swore that she would never again tag after Amanda and firmly planted herself in front of the TV, with her laptop and cell phone close at hand.

A day later, Amanda and Josie met at the County Historical Society archives, in the basement of the Maysville Library, and scanned through rolls of microfilm for old newspaper articles from August 1912.

"There it is!" Amanda pointed to the headline of the small article illuminated on the screen: "Band of Gypsies on Rampage."

It began: "The public is warned that a band of colorfully dressed gypsies is operating in town, breaking into family homes and attacking innocent people. They are skilled in the arts of illusion...."

"That is so weird!" Josie gasped. "They're writing about us."

"That means this article was here all the time!" Amanda said to her friend. "It was in the historical documents. So we just had to go back to confirm, not change, history."

"Maybe the article didn't appear until we went back in time and then returned," Josie said. "We can't know for sure."

"That's even weirder," Amanda said.

"All I can say," Josie muttered, "is that I'm gobsmacked."

Amanda's eyes gleamed as she read through the piece. "Just like most newspaper articles, they sure got a lot of the facts wrong."

"Whatever the explanation, we did go back in history and everything turned out well for Jan and Katie. And for us," Josie agreed.

That afternoon, despite her solemn vow never to return to the Tucker house, Roxanne ventured over. Sally pried her eyes away from the television, and the girls all hung out together. Shortly after lunch, they drifted to sleep in the living room, where Tulip had been snoozing away the morning under the end table.

Exhausted after the long, terrifying night, Amanda dreamed about traveling back in time again, except that she and her sister and friends arrived in the dazzling light of midday. They were walking down their own street when they glimpsed Clement and Mabel Blackburn climbing into a buggy to which a horse had been harnessed. It appeared to be the same horse that had shied away from the man while he was beating Jan Brandowski. The horse fidgeted when Judge Blackburn slapped the reins across its back, but settled into a trot. Amanda didn't know where the man and his wife were headed, perhaps downtown to do a little shopping at the mercantile, to the judge's office, or simply on a Sunday drive.

It appeared that everything in Maysville had been sweet and pleasant, or maybe that was how people had always viewed the past. Maybe a charming veneer had always covered the dark secrets of some people—the disdain and violence toward immigrants, minorities, and other poor people.

Amanda was relieved when she surfaced through the layers of sleep. Josie and Roxanne were rubbing their eyes while Sally was already multi-tasking on her laptop—emailing friends, playing a game, and checking St. Louis Cardinals baseball scores on a website—and playing a videogame on their television.

"You girls must have been up late," Mr. Tucker joked as he sauntered into the room. "It's dinnertime already."

"Are you hungry, girls?" Liddy Tucker asked as she strolled in from the kitchen.

Mr. Tucker had grilled hamburgers and hot dogs, which Liddy placed on the dining room table, with a mountain of homemade French fries, dill pickles, and condiments—mustard, catsup, and horseradish that Sally liked on just about all her food.

"Yuck," Amanda said as she watched her sister slather a mix of condiments on a charbroiled hamburger and two hot dogs.

Tulip had devoured another bowl of dog chow. She now squatted by the dining room table and eyed the charbroiled meats in hopes that some delectable morsel would fall on the floor, or someone would take pity on a sad little dog and slip her a greasy hot dog or juicy hamburger.

Soon, all the fare had been consumed by humans—with a little help from one hungry hound.

After stuffing themselves and Tulip, the girls decided to take a stroll around the park. Amanda didn't even complain when

Sally tagged along. They wandered over to the pavilion, noting what had changed and what had endured over the decades in their old neighborhood. They chatted a little, but, overwhelmed by the events of last night, they often lapsed into silent awe.

As the veil of dusk settled over them, they noticed an elderly man, walking a Jack Russell terrier along the sidewalk. As the frisky little dog sniffed for rabbits in the bushes and yapped at squirrels scrambling up trees, the old man muttered, "This way, Scamp."

"Hey, that's old Pete Brandowski. He must be Katie and John's son," Roxanne said, fitting the pieces of the puzzle together. "Maybe he was their first child after they eloped."

They had often seen the sweet old man walking his little dog in the park, but had never thought much about it—until now.

"And Pete is you-know-who's grandfather," Josie teased with a glimmer in her eye. "John Brandowski—your true love, Amanda!"

"He is *not* my true love," Amanda insisted, blushing roses. *At least not yet,* she thought, because she did have a huge crush on John. Of course, she knew better than to *ever* admit that to her friends. There'd be no end to their ribbing.

"John doesn't even know I'm alive," she mumbled.

"I wouldn't be so sure," Josie said. "He's always making those gooey eyes at you."

Amanda squirmed. "He is not!"

Roxanne chanted, "Amanda and John sitting in a tree, k-i-s-s-i-n-g."

Josie and Sally chimed in.

"Knock it off," Amanda cried. "You are all *so* immature."

They laughed, of course, but then became thoughtfully quiet, and Roxanne couldn't help sighing, "John *is* cute."

That prompted Sally to declare, "Boys are disgusting."

"John is more than cute," Josie contended. "He's dreamy."

Sally made gagging noises.

Amanda, Josie, and Roxanne smiled at each other.

"I pity the guy who falls for you, Sally," Josie kidded. "He's going to have his hands full."

The old man ambled over to them, and the girls knelt and petted the bright-eyed terrier with its pink tongue hanging out, delighted with all the attention.

"You are the girls?" the old man asked.

The girls looked up in surprise. Then, one by one, they stood up.

He raised his bushy white eyebrows. "And you have the cameo brooch?"

Amanda had almost forgotten the heirloom. "Yes!" she said breathlessly. "How on earth did you know?"

The old man shrugged. "My father often told a story of some strange girls who came back in time, how they helped Katie and him. He told us how Katie had lost her treasured piece of jewelry, but from the train he saw one of the girls pick it up. He always said he had a feeling that someday the brooch might come back to our family."

Amanda dug into her pocket and gave the cameo to him.

"It has been in good hands," the old man said.

"Yes," Amanda whispered.

The old man smiled. "I had hoped that someday the cameo would find its way back to us. My father was always certain that it would, that it must. Over the generations, it has been lost and found many times, as wars ravaged our old country. It is the oval of life, since none of us are perfectly round, my father always said. It is too late for Katie, but that cameo should be passed to another generation. I will give the cameo to my grandson, who will someday give it to his bride."

The old man's eyes sparkled as he gazed at Amanda. "And who knows who that may be."

"But how did you know *we* were those girls?" Josie asked.

"I didn't. Not at first. But you told me, in the way you were looking at me just now," the old man said.

The old man bid them farewell, and the girls watched as Pete Brandowski strolled out of the park, crossed Elm Street, and disappeared around the corner with his little dog.

"Grandson?" Josie asked. "Do you suppose he means John?"

"I bet John is named after his great-grandfather," Roxanne mused.

Amanda gulped. "Maybe."

Roxanne wriggled her shoulders. "You could, like, ask him sometime."

"Maybe," Amanda answered, feeling the heat rise in her face.

"Hey, guys, I've got a great idea!" Josie exclaimed. "We can have another sleepover—tonight. We can try to go through the mirror again."

Sally instantly froze.

"Are you crazy?" Roxanne cried. "I'm never going back in time, not ever again."

"Who said 'back'? Maybe the mirror will let us travel forward in time," Josie said. "We can see the future. How about that?"

Sally and Roxanne were too shocked to answer her.

"What makes you think that the mirror would let us?" Amanda asked.

Josie shrugged. "We'll never know until we try. Think about it. If we can travel into the future, we can see if Amanda really marries John Brandowski someday."

"Yeah, maybe you'll have the cameo," Roxanne kidded, "and live happily ever after. Wouldn't you like to know your future?"

"No thanks," Amanda said. "I'd rather live one day at a time and see what happens."

Of course…it would be nice to get to know John Brandowski better in the here and now, she thought. *After all, he comes from such a nice family.*

THE END

About the Author

RAYMOND BIAL is the acclaimed author of more than 100 books for children and adults, including many historical photo-documentary books such as *Amish Home, The Underground Railroad, Where Lincoln Walked, A Handful of Dirt, Tenement, Nauvoo, Ellis Island, Rescuing Rover,* and others. The list includes more than two dozen books about Native American peoples.

His books have received many awards from the American Library Association, Children's Book Council, and many other organizations.

His other books of ghost stories include *The Fresh Grave, The Ghost of Honeymoon Creek, Dripping Blood Cave,* and *Shadow Island.*

He lives in Urbana, Illinois.